Please Don't Go

A Short Story Trilogy
By: Tesa Erven

Copyright © 2020

ISBN: *9781096443872*

Cover: Humbird Media
Editor: Paulette Nunlee, Five Star Proofing

Note from the Author:

In February 2019, I had the pleasure of visiting the ladies of Divine Eyes Book Club for the fourth time to share with them the final installment in *The Loose End* Series. It was a day filled with joy as they presented me with a beautiful engraved pen and journal. At the time, I had no idea what to write next or if I would even write again. It wasn't until a week later when tragedy struck and we were mourning the death of Tara Myers, one of the book club members. Needless to say, we took her passing hard and that's when I felt compelled to write the *Please Don't Go* trilogy. Little did I know part one would make it on Amazon's bestseller list in May 2019. With that being said, I'm truly grateful for my writing journey. Despite the life-changing experiences we all go through, I hope that you will continue to enjoy reading about imperfect characters as much as I enjoy writing about them.

Love and Hugs, T

DEDICATION

In Loving Memory of Tara, Divine Eyes Book
Club Member. We miss you.

Blessed are those who mourn,
for they will be comforted.

Matthew 5:4

Part One
Table of Contents

IN PLAIN SIGHT

Present Day

Vanessa walked into her office on a rainy Saturday afternoon. Normally, she didn't come in on weekends, but she cancelled her original plans of attending the wedding of Sonya St. Jermaine and Dray McKinnis. Her excuse: she suddenly felt ill and declined the invite at the last minute. Perhaps, her feeling of nausea was because Bradsen Myers, a man she'd previously dated, was going to be there with her former client—his new wife. However, that was a while ago in *What Could've Been*. Since then, that ship had sailed. Although, her brief time with Bradsen helped tremendously because as a parting gift, he'd paid off the lease agreement for the year to her practice. She was able to hire her much-needed assistant, Lisa Pierce.

Lisa was a single, thirty-year-old African American woman with wild natural curly hair, light smooth skin and adorable dimples. She had a bachelor's degree in psychology and worked as a case manager in healthcare providing advice and counseling to people in difficult situations. Before going to work for Vanessa, her former position was great until her female boss began to make sexual advances. The feeling wasn't mutual, so things soon became uncomfortable for Lisa. Embarrassed and tired of evading Sarah's wandering hands and tripping over her feet trying to reclaim her space, she lost her patience. Sarah's act of innocence to

Lisa's requests to "leave me alone" was just too much. The last straw. She was having her own #*me too* moment. It was at that point she decided to resign from the hospital rather than reporting the harassment to HR. While job hunting, she came across Vanessa's listing posted with other announcements in the hospital's lounge area. Lisa had reservations about working for another woman, but Vanessa assured her that she would be fine. Her place of business wasn't a hookup site. In time, the two began to bond after realizing they had a lot in common and soon became good friends.

"Hi, Lisa, what are you doing here?" Vanessa was surprised to see her in the office.

"Hey, Vanessa." Lisa looked up from her computer. "I'm here to check on my 'sick friend'," she said, using air quotes to suggest otherwise.

Vanessa laughed and pulled off her coat. "I should've never told you that story."

"I'm just saying," Lisa shrugged, "you look fine to me." Vanessa was dressed business casual in a pair of slacks, collared blouse and flat black shoes.

"Oh, no you don't..." Lisa watched her turn on her tablet preparing to settle in at her desk. "We are not staying in this office on a Saturday. There's no reason for us to be here."

"I can't. I have a lot to do," Vanessa whined. There was always one of her clients who expected her to answer emails on any given day.

"Since when?" Lisa raised a brow. "Thanks to me, your workload is stable." That was true. Thanks to Lisa who answered the phones, greeted clients, organized files and took on some of the less demanding cases.

She was more than an assistant; they made a great team.

"So, before you get too comfortable... Come on, I'll treat you to lunch."

"That won't be necessary, Lisa."

"Don't do that."

"Do what?"

"If I want to treat you to lunch, just say okay."

"Okay," Vanessa said in a mocking tone. "Where would you like to go?"

"I was thinking we could go to the Marriott Union Square on Sutter Street. I hear they have a nice grilled salmon I've been wanting to try."

"Sounds good," Vanessa agreed, as they headed out the door.

* * *

Sincere Lewis pulled his eighteen-wheeler truck into the back of the Marriott Hotel, directly to the dock entrance. Deliveries were usually scheduled on weekdays during business hours, but heavy rains on the east coast had delayed his driving across a few states. Luckily, he had a great relationship with Antonio, the hotel general manager, and was able to make special arrangements to deliver his load today.

Sincere owned his own trucking company, Lewis Transport Services (LTS). His truck, with a built-in refrigeration system, hauled and kept food products in their pre-shipped state. Some of his products and goods specialized in high-end meats: USDA prime, Kobe beef, filet mignon and various steaks such as New York strip, T-bone and porterhouse.

Sincere took over the family business shortly after his dad died of pancreatic cancer. He personally wanted to be a big-time chef like his idol Gordon Ramsey, who owned and operated a series of restaurants. But as fate would have it, as an only child, he felt obligated to step in and continue his father's legacy. He was in his late twenties at the time of his dad's passing which devastated him and his mom in a way that he couldn't put into words. They were very close, but his heartbroken mother couldn't take living in the family home any longer. So, she moved to New Jersey to start a new life. For Sincere, he remained in Atlanta because he couldn't sell his dad's trucking company. Or the house he had worked so hard to build. Eventually, the assets he inherited were transferred into his name and he made it his own.

Sincere walked through the dock entrance doors and greeted Antonio with a fist-bump. After small talk, Antonio signed the receiving papers and Sincere carefully guided the liftgate down to the ground. He moved the freight with his manual pallet jack and pushed it onto the service elevator. Upon returning to his truck, he stopped short when he recognized a familiar face walking towards the hotel.

* * *

"Sin..." Vanessa said, as shock registered across her face. She slowed her pace.

"Yes, girl, he is *sinfully* handsome." Lisa admired the sight of the gentleman standing at a distance in front of them. At nearly six feet, Sincere was an attractive black man with an athletic figure, short cropped wavy hair, dark eyes and a baby face that made him appear younger than he was. His large, well-defined muscles were revealed in the short-sleeve shirt he wore paired with ripped jeans and work boots.

"Too bad I'm not into light skinned men or else I would be all over him. But what about you? He seems like your type." Lisa nudged her elbow. "It would be a sin if you don't go over there and talk to him."

"Huh?" Vanessa said, snapping out of her trance. "No, Lisa, that's his name... Sincere Lewis. I know him."

"Oh really, you do?" Lisa raised a brow. "Do I dare ask?"

Vanessa shook her head. "He's someone from my past. It was a long time ago."

"Well considering you've only been in San Francisco for about a year, how long is long?"

"Let's just keep walking. If we're lucky, he won't see us. Although, your drooling over him—I'm pretty sure—gave us away," Vanessa teased.

"Whatever." Lisa laughed.

* * *

Sincere pulled off and stored his protective gloves once he spotted the woman who had invaded his dreams for the past months. She hadn't changed a bit. Tall, slender beauty with dark brown skin and jet-black hair. He'd thought about her often. He knew she left Atlanta and relocated to San Francisco to pursue a business opportunity. However, it remained a mystery to him where in the city she'd gone. Seeing her brought back a lot of painful memories, unspoken emotions and time lost. Their undeniable chemistry had shaken them both to the core, causing her to run away, and he was forced to let her go. At the time, his life had been turned upside down and the thought of being with someone else–it wasn't going to happen anytime soon.

He kept watching until she got closer. *Is she really going to walk past me and not speak?*

Vanessa reached out to push the door to enter the hotel. He quickly rushed over before she could open it.

"Doctor Vanessa Stevens. I know you see me."

Vanessa stopped, briefly closed her eyes and let out a deep breath. She appeared to be speechless.

"Well, if she doesn't see you, I sure do." Lisa spoke up and said in a flirtatious tone, "Hi, I'm her assistant, Lisa Pierce, and you are?" She extended her hand to him.

"Hi, Sincere Lewis," he said, as they exchanged handshakes.

"I take it you and Vanessa know each other," she inquired.

"Yes, it's been a while, but we met in Atlanta."

"Oh...okay, nice." Lisa glanced over at Vanessa. "I'll give you two a minute to catch up. We can meet inside."

Vanessa finally found her voice. "There's no need. I'm coming."

She gave Sincere a piercing glance. "Hello, Sincere, I see you. And now I don't. Continue to have a nice life." Vanessa turned her back on him and walked away from the door as she pulled Lisa along with her.

"Whoa!" Lisa said. She stopped, her mouth hung open in disbelief. "I have never seen you lose your cool like that. Ever. And I thought Bradsen Myers hurt you, but this other guy has nothing on him. What in the hell did he do?"

"Girl, don't let his handsome features fool you. Sincere is not so sincere."

"Is that so?"

They turned abruptly when he quietly walked up behind them, overhearing a portion of their conversation. "Why? Because I didn't beg you to stay in Atlanta?"

Vanessa's face was a struggle to keep her composure. "No, because you let me go. And you and I both know what that meant."

Sincere didn't say a word.

"Yeah, I thought that would shut you up," she spat.

Vanessa turned her attention to Lisa. "Come on, Lisa, I'm not even hungry anymore. Let's get out of here."

Vanessa started to move, but Sincere gently grabbed her hand. The instant spark they once had suddenly reappeared.

"Please don't go," he said above a whisper. "Can we go somewhere and talk?"

Vanessa rolled her eyes. "It's been over a year and you're finally ready to talk?" She threw up her hands. "Look—"

"Maybe this isn't the time or place." Lisa interrupted her before she could say more. Other patrons entering the restaurant were beginning to take notice of their actions outside the prestigious establishment.

"You're right." Vanessa lowered her voice. She reached inside her designer handbag, pulled out her business card and handed it to Sincere. "Since you're ready to talk, you can call my office and schedule an appointment." Vanessa stomped away.

"It was nice meeting you, I guess," Lisa said, following closely behind Vanessa.

* * *

Vanessa and Lisa walked over to Bush Street to Akiko's, a nice, charming sushi bar. The restaurant offered a modern décor with a touch of Japanese flare. The dinner crowd hadn't arrived yet, so the friendly waitstaff was able to seat them right away. Lisa requested a booth near the back so she could hear all about Sincere Lewis and why he wasn't so sincere. Once the waiter greeted them, Vanessa ordered plum wine and pan-fried gyoza while Lisa wanted some sake and a California roll. After the waiter left, Lisa told her to spill the beans.

"How long do you have?"

"All day and night if need be," Lisa joked.

"In that case, we're going to need stronger drinks," Vanessa said and signaled again for their waiter as she began to reminisce on how she met Sincere Lewis when she lived in Atlanta.

15

* * *

Meanwhile, back at the Marriott Hotel, Sincere was having those same exact thoughts as Antonio offered him to stay and grab a bite to eat together before getting on the road. As he sat there in silence, his mind wandered to what happened just over a year ago.

GONE TOO SOON

One Year Ago

After driving across country, Sincere was ready to return home to Tara, the love of his life. Earlier that day, she'd called him because she wasn't feeling well. She left her nursing job early complaining of a headache. He told her to take something and lie down and that he would be home to see her soon. "Love you" were the last words spoken to each other before they ended the call.

It was shortly after midnight when Sincere entered their three-bedroom home in Snellville. East of Atlanta, Snellville was considered a suburb in Gwinnett County. Their charming home offered hardwood floors that led directly into a spacious kitchen that featured granite countertops, cherrywood cabinets and stainless-steel appliances. The two-story structure also had two and half baths, a large living room, family room and master bedroom.

He dropped his belongings at the stairs and made his way into the kitchen to pour himself a drink. He already knew Tara would be asleep for the night, so he took a few moments to unwind while looking through the stack of mail on the counter. There were a couple of bills, but for the most part, it was mostly junk. Once he was done, he noticed a sticky note: *Sin, I left you a plate of food in the fridge.* He smiled. Tara took such good care of him.

He and Tara met by chance five years ago. They had a strong connection and began dating shortly thereafter. It didn't take long for Sincere to realize that she was the *one*. Her beautiful spirit filled the room along with her bright smile across her rich, dark brown face. He was hooked. Six months later, they were married. Everything happened so fast, but they didn't care about what others thought. They were in love. Life was good, and he couldn't wait to fill their home with kids someday. Sincere crept up the stairs and slowly opened the bedroom door. He stopped short. Something was off. Tara was lying on top of the bed, still in her work scrubs. Thinking she was just tired, he walked over to her side and whispered, "Tara, baby, I'm home. You okay?" Tara didn't move.

"Baby?" Sincere went to lightly shake her awake, and that's when he got the shock of his life. His eyes grew wide in horror. His heart started to race.

"Come on, Tara. Wake up, baby. This shit is not funny," he said as he began to panic.

"TARA!" he shouted, but it was no use. Tara's lifeless body lay there resting in peace. He screamed and cried out before gaining enough strength to dial 9-1-1. In the blink of an eye, his world came crashing down. Following the coroner's investigation, it was confirmed that at age thirty-one, Tara Lewis died from an aneurysm.

* * *

Days, weeks and then months went by in a blur. Nearing a year and Sincere still walked around feeling like a zombie. Constant replays of the screams of anguish and sorrow from the calls to her mother and friends interrupted his sleeping moments. His symptoms increased to depression, feelings of sadness and hopelessness. In his mind, he had nothing left to live for. Life without Tara had no meaning.

He picked up the keys to his SUV. Already sleep-deprived, he had no business getting behind the wheel. He started the engine anyway and drove off into the early morning, staring straight ahead on an empty highway. His visual image continuously fading through heavy tears. As objects moved quickly past his eyes, trees kept getting larger and larger. Suddenly, he was losing control of the vehicle...

* * *

Vanessa was sitting in her shared office space that she rented on Century Boulevard. As a new business owner, it was a great location with direct access to two major interstates convenient to Buckhead,

Midtown, and Downtown. It featured a glass atrium with a contemporary design, wood paneling and custom artwork. Through the window was a small pond that surrounded the commercial building. The office was the right size and just what she needed for her clients to feel at ease. Not to mention, it was within budget that was split between her and a few other therapists. They each had a set day to use the space. It worked for now, but her goal was to have her own office one day. Shortly after her arrival, the phone rang.

"Hello. This is Dr. Stevens. How can I help you?"

"Hi, Dr. Stevens. This is Dr. Rebecca Donnelly over at Piedmont Hospital." Rebecca Donnelly was a board-certified doctor who Vanessa met at a networking event. They exchanged business cards and set up a face-to-face meet. Despite their different ethnic backgrounds, they instantly hit it off.

Soon after, Dr. Donnelly called often to refer new patients.

"We have a possible suicidal patient. African-American male. Early thirties. Police report shows that his truck crashed into a guardrail on Highway 78."

Vanessa gasped. "Is he okay?"

"He's lucky to be alive, but he's mourning the death of his wife who recently passed away. Can you take the case?"

Vanessa sighed. Grief therapy was always hard. Because how do you find the right words to say? Especially when someone is traumatized. Her job would be to help him cope by taking it one day at a time.

"Thank you, Dr. Donnelly, for referring me. Leave the papers at the nurses' station and I'll see what I can do." Vanessa released the call.

* * *

Sincere woke up in Piedmont's hospital bed with non-life-threatening injuries. Some bruising across his chest and abdomen from the seatbelt. A few scrapes from the damaged windshield. Thankfully, his airbag had functioned properly or things could've been a lot worse. Dr. Donnelly said his mother had been notified and would be arriving soon from New Jersey.

Sincere blew out an exasperated breath. "I wish you hadn't done that."

Dr. Donnelly raised a brow. "Well given the circumstances, we had no other choice. You were unconscious."

"Yeah, but my family's been through a lot already."

"I understand. Which is another reason why I think you should talk to someone."

"Talk to someone?" he said, perplexed. "Like who? I feel okay. When can I get out of here?"

"Well, not quite. You're here under observation. Do you remember anything about the accident?"

Truthfully, the only thing Sincere could remember was wanting to see Tara again. "No, not really."

"Okay, well, I'm going to run a few more tests, and if everything checks out, we'll release you then."

After no response, Dr. Donnelly continued, "Get some rest. Dr. Vanessa Stevens will be here to speak with you soon."

"Wait, doctor..." He stopped her. "I really don't need to talk to anyone. It was just late. I was tired and..." Sincere's voice started to crack while he held back tears.

She must have sensed his stress. It was clear in her eyes. "No worries, Mr. Lewis, you have to be patient with yourself. You need time to heal both physically and mentally. No matter what you're going through, better days are ahead if you keep moving forward." She touched his arm.

"I'll be back to check on you later," Dr. Donnelly said, as she walked out the room.

* * *

All visitors needed to obtain a visitor's pass from the hospital information desk in the main building lobby prior to visiting patients. Vanessa filled out the necessary information and then made her way to the elevators. She pressed the button, waited for the doors to open and stepped inside. Once the doors closed, she said a silent prayer that she would be able to help out her latest client. She always said she couldn't save them all, but if she could help one, she was making a difference. The elevator came to a complete stop on the floor she needed and she headed to the nurses' station. Cheryl, the registered nurse sitting there, handed her a file and Vanessa skimmed through the documents. For some reason, she was nervous. She'd helped numerous people in the past, but this case felt different. Maybe because her client's life was hanging in the balance after his wife's untimely death. She tucked the file away in her tote bag and slid her sweaty palms across her slacks. She tapped on the door before gently pushing it open.

"Hello, Mr. Lewis, I'm Dr. Vanessa Stevens." She stepped into the room.

Sincere was lying in bed with his head tilted to the side, staring blankly out the window. She cleared her throat to get his attention. He slowly turned his head to face her. His dark eyes appeared to be puffy from a lack of sleep.

"Hello," was all he said and turned his head back towards the window. Despite the flutter in her stomach, Vanessa remained cool. She knew he wouldn't be receptive to her words. She would have to take a different approach.

"You mind if I have a seat?" she asked.

Sincere shrugged.

"I'll take that as a yes." Vanessa grabbed an empty chair by the door. The sound of the chair against the floor could be heard clearly because of the silence in the room. She placed it in front of the window next to his bed. Sincere shook his head but still hadn't said a word. As they sat in total silence, thirty minutes passed.

"Well, that was refreshing," Vanessa said. "Same time tomorrow?" She glanced at him and raised an eyebrow.

Sincere didn't make any gestures at all. He just smirked, and Vanessa took that as a sign she was getting somewhere.

A HELPING HAND

"Sincere? There's my baby." Sincere's mother, Doreen Lewis, rushed into the hospital room. A beautiful older woman, she was short and light-skinned with natural low-cut hair. She was casually dressed in comfortable shoes, boot-cut jeans, a sweater set, along with her signature gold cross necklace that she always wore. Her dark-brown eyes were filled with tears as she hurried to his side.

"Oh, my God." She covered her mouth. "Look at you," she cried when she saw the scratches and bruises on his face. "What happened to you?" She leaned over him and hugged him tight. "The doctor said you were in some kind of car accident."

"Hi, Ma. I'm okay. You didn't have to come."

"Like hell I didn't. You're my one and only. If something would've happened to you... I can't lose you too..." She was too upset to continue. Wiping tears away with tissue, she asked, "Where's your doctor? Has she been here to see you yet?"

"Not yet. But she should be here soon. I'm ready to go home," he said with an attitude.

"Home? Are you sure? Maybe you need a little more time... I mean... just to be sure."

"Ma, I'm fine," he snapped at her.

"You are not fine," she retorted. "But, whatever you say. Because I'm not here to argue with you... If you want to—" Doreen

31

stopped talking when Dr. Donnelly walked in.

"Hello. I'm Dr. Donnelly and you must be Mrs. Lewis?" They shook hands.

"Yes. How's my boy doing?" Doreen asked.

"Well, as you know he was involved in a serious car crash. All his tests came back normal, so on the surface his overall health is good. However, as I mentioned to Sincere, I am concerned about his state of mind and recommended that he speak to a therapist."

"A therapist?" Doreen repeated. She knew her son all too well, and that wasn't going to happen. Just like she was raised, she taught him to keep his problems to himself. You handled it one of two ways. You either prayed about it or you drank about it. And when her husband, Sincere Sr. died, she was no different. She relied on alcohol to cope with the tragedy.

Dr. Donnelly said, "I understand people have their own methods on how to deal with tragic situations, but I'm afraid if Sincere doesn't get the proper help, he may not be so lucky next time."

"How dare you say that?" Doreen quickly responded. No matter how bad the situation was, no parent wanted to hear the truth about their child.

"I don't mean to upset you. It's just my opinion, and I already referred him to talk to someone."

Dr. Donnelly turned her attention to Sincere. "How are you feeling?"

"Much better."

"Okay. Well, since you're feeling better, you'll be discharged later today. Remember what I said. Take care of yourself."

"Thank you, Doctor." Sincere said, as Dr. Donnelly excused herself and left the room.

* * *

"Ma, I got it," Sincere said, reaching for the small bag in the backseat. She parked the rental car in front of his driveway.

"Are you sure? Why don't you come back to the hotel with me? I can take care of you there."

"Nah, I'm good." Sincere preferred to be at home. In his own bed. "Besides, you chose to stay in a hotel when you know there is plenty of space here."

"I know, it's just that..." she waved it off.

"What, Ma? It's been five years since you've stepped foot into this house. How can you say you've moved on and still have issues with the past? That doesn't make sense to me."

"Boy, mind your business! This isn't about me. I'm here for you. But if you keep talking shit..." She started the car.

Sincere apologized. It had been a long, exhausting day. Right now, all he wanted to do was go inside and get some rest.

"Okay, well do you need anything?" His mother softened her tone.

"No, but thanks for picking up my prescription and buying some food. This should last me until tomorrow."

Doreen was hesitant to leave her son, but she couldn't bear the thought of going inside her old home. "Love you, Sin."

"Love you, too. I'll call you later."

* * *

Sincere walked into his empty home. There was an eerie feeling as he looked around the room. Everything he saw reminded him of Tara. From the living room décor to the master bedroom. When she moved in, she'd remodeled the entire house. He agreed because his parents old-fashioned taste didn't match their modern style. He went into the kitchen to put away the food. He wasn't hungry. So instead, he reached for the prescribed pills and a bottle of Jack Daniel's and headed up the stairs.

Should I do it, he asked himself. He held the items in his hand. After two days of not getting enough sleep, Sincere began to hallucinate as he sank to the floor in his bedroom. He believed he saw Tara standing there.

"Baby, there you are." He smiled at the shadowy figure. "I looked around for

you everywhere but couldn't find you. Why did you leave me?" He started to cry.

"I didn't leave you. I'm right here with you always," Tara's image responded.

"Baby, I can't do this without you. I miss you so much." He sobbed louder. "How about I just take all these pills and join you? We can be together again."

"We'll be together again, but right now it was my time to go. Please stay and take care of your mom. She needs you."

"But I need you. I love you, Tara."

He stretched his arms as the shadowy figure began to fade. Instead of taking the pills, he cried himself to sleep.

* * *

Vanessa didn't usually make house calls. Not because she couldn't, it was more for the lack of privacy and safety concerns.

Since it wasn't her environment, she couldn't control any issues that might escalate. She showed up at the hospital, but to her surprise, Sincere had been discharged the day before. As a follow-up, she took it upon herself to drive to his home to see if he were okay. She parked a few feet away, got out and made her way up to the door. She noticed an older woman sitting alone in a parked car in front of his driveway. Vanessa walked over and lightly tapped on the glass.

The woman rolled down her window. "Can I help you?"

"Yes, I'm Dr. Vanessa Stevens looking for Sincere Lewis. Do you know if he's home?"

The woman had a faraway look on her face. "I don't know," she admitted. "He won't answer the phone."

"Did you try ringing the doorbell?" Vanessa was confused.

The woman appeared frazzled and was crying. "I don't have to. I'm his mother, Doreen Lewis, I used to live here."

Now that she knew the woman's identity that explained a lot. But why was she acting like she had lost her best friend? Little did Vanessa know, she had. Thinking the worst, Vanessa blurted out, "Has something happened to Sincere? Should I call the police?" She pulled out her phone.

Doreen shook her head. "No, I just can't bring myself to go into the house. Too many painful memories."

What is she talking about? Clearly, she came to help Sincere, but it seemed his mom was in pretty bad shape, too. Vanessa could only focus her attention on one person at a time.

"Mrs. Lewis, I need to make sure Sincere is okay. I'll be right back." Vanessa stepped away from the car. She quickly made her way to the door and rang the bell.

* * *

Sincere stirred awake as he heard the ringing in his ear. He focused around the room, daylight peeking through the curtains. The unopened liquor and bottle of pills were beside him. After a few moments, it hit him like a ton of bricks; he was prepared to take his own life. He sat up to gather his thoughts when the ringing started again. It finally registered that someone was at the door. *Who could it be?* he thought, as he shifted his body forward to stand. Although his mom was in town and had a spare key, she was too afraid to come over, let alone use it. He quickly went into the bathroom to splash some water on his face and brush his teeth. He went downstairs and opened the door. He widened his eyes, then narrowed them. "What are you doing here?" He redirected his attention over her shoulders. "Ma?" Before he could say more, his mother started the car and sped away. Sincere just shook his head.

Wide-eyed, Vanessa's frown registered confusion. She shook her head, then answered his question. "I went by the hospital earlier today, but you were gone. I thought I would stop by and check on you. We didn't get to talk much yesterday." She attempted a joke.

"Is that part of your job?" he asked snidely.

Vanessa bit her lower lip and looked down at her shaking hands.

"Doesn't matter," he softened his voice. "I'm actually glad you're here. I could use your help." After last night's incident, he knew he needed to seek help. He opened the door wider and invited her inside.

* * *

Once inside, Vanessa surveyed his place. She was very observant when it came to her surroundings. It didn't take long for her to realize she was standing in his childhood home. Family portraits on the wall. A few handmade antiques. Although, the furniture had been updated, there was something about a mother's unique sense of style and it showed in the china cabinet that lined the dining room wall. The formal dishes were neatly arranged, stacked on top of each other. Most young couples today had no clue what that was. But, in her home when she was growing up, it meant something special. Especially around the holidays. Her mother would pull out what was affectionately known as the "good china."

Sincere came up beside her. "It belongs to my mom. It was the one piece that I wouldn't let my wife get rid of. It's funny because I remember her asking me, 'what does it do?'

"Nothing was my reply. It just sits there and collects dust." He smiled.

Vanessa kept him talking. "Did your mom have the matching tablecloth and napkins, too?"

"Of course. We couldn't eat without it. She used to..." His facial expression changed.

Vanessa recognized the look. He wasn't ready to share. So, she quickly switched topics. "You know what? I'm thirsty. May I have something to drink?"

"Oh, shoot, where are my manners? Right this way." Sincere led her to the kitchen and poured her some juice.

Vanessa admired all the fancy cookware. "Wow! Are you a chef?"

"No, I'm a truck driver. But I think you knew that, and you're just doing your job to distract me."

"Is it working?"

"It depends."

"On what?"

"On whether I see you again."

Vanessa blushed. She didn't mean to, but his witty response caught her off guard. She knew it wasn't meant to be said in a flirtatious tone. Although it sure sounded that way.

Okay, don't get too comfortable, she told herself. *Maybe I should leave.* She didn't want to wear out her welcome. "Well I hate to drink and run." She returned the glass. "But it looks like our time is up."

"Really? That's a shame because talking to you was better than I thought," Sincere admitted.

She was pleased to hear that.

"So, how can I get you to eat and stay?" he challenged.

"Next time," Vanessa said, "but only on one condition..."

"Yeah, and what's that?"

"You have to treat me to a home-cooked meal in your fancy pots."

Sincere laughed for the first time in a long time. "You have yourself a deal," he agreed to the terms as he walked her out.

* * *

Doreen entered her hotel room at the Hampton Inn & Suites with a solemn look upon her face. *That didn't go as planned*, she thought. She slumped into an empty chair.

The other person sitting there moved towards Doreen. "Are you okay? How did it go?"

"Truthfully," Doreen cried, "this is harder than I thought. Sincere got out the hospital yesterday, and I still haven't found the right time to have a real conversation with him. I tried to go over to his house like we'd talked about, but I still couldn't get out the car. It was scary, and then, what really freaked me out was he had a therapist show up."

"Really? Sincere's been through so much lately, that may be a good thing."

Doreen shrugged and said, "Maybe."

"Now if only you could tell him about me, so we can confront your past and move forward," the person said, concerned, and returned to their seat.

BETWEEN US

Sincere picked up Vanessa's business card for the third time and stared at the number. He hadn't heard from her in a few days and wanted to hear her voice. It was now or never to do this while he still had the nerve. He dialed the number. She answered on the first ring.

"Hello. This is Dr. Stevens. How can I help you?"

Sincere hesitated before answering. *Maybe I should hang up?* "Hello?"

"Dr. Stevens, this is Sincere Lewis," he whispered.

"Hi, Sincere, it's good to hear from you." Vanessa sounded upbeat.

"I was wondering...if you were free for dinner tonight. If you want? Just an invite. We could talk some more." Sincere started to ramble.

"I would love to. Is five o'clock, good? I can come right over when I leave work."

Sincere could envision her smile through the phone and knew she could sense his nervousness. "That's fine. See you soon."

* * *

Sincere was preparing garlic braised short ribs that he placed in a slow cooker. For flavoring, he added onion, celery, carrots and salt and pepper and cooked it slowly until the short ribs were tender, falling off the bone. *Perfect,* he thought. He could've served it right out the pot, however, he transferred the short ribs to a dinner plate with mashed potatoes and a salad on the side. He paired the dish with a nice red wine.

"So, what do you think?" Sincere asked, curious. They were having an early dinner.

"Mmmm," her mouth full, "it's sooo good."

"Thank you." He smiled. Something he found himself doing a lot more.

"Do I taste a little bit of lemon zest?"

"Let me find out you know your stuff." He was impressed.

"I know a little something but not like this..." She pointed at her plate. "This belongs in a cookbook.

"Did your wife cook?" Vanessa knew to tread lightly. Although, she'd been spending time with Sincere, he still hadn't quite opened up to her.

"No, but she could microwave." They both laughed.

"You know what I've been meaning to ask? How's your mom doing? She had me worried the other day. She was so afraid to get out the car."

"Yeah, I know. Ever since my dad died, she hasn't stepped foot into this house."

"Don't you find that kind of strange?"

"I do, but I have my own issues. Isn't that the reason why you're here?"

The look on her face told him she knew she'd walked right into that one.

"Are you ready for dessert?" he asked, getting up from the table.

"You bake, too?" Vanessa said excitedly. "Where have you been all my life?"

An instant silence filled the room. It was a déjà vu moment for him because those were the same exact words that Tara used when he first cooked for her.

"Sincere, I'm sorry that was so unprofessional of me." Vanessa sank back in her chair.

"Don't worry about it." He stepped away to bring out chocolate fudge brownies. When he returned, he leaned over her shoulder. "If you think dinner was good, wait until you taste dessert," he said, breaking the awkward silence between them.

* * *

"Thank you, Sincere. Everything was delicious," Vanessa said. They were sitting in the family room having an after-dinner drink. "Where did you learn how to cook?"

"Well, when I graduated high school, I stayed local and went to Gwinnett Technical College where I studied culinary arts. It wasn't until my dad got sick, I gave up cooking classes and switched to their automotive program to learn what I could about diesel engines and operating heavy equipment. I wanted to help out, because I thought Dad would get better. It never dawned on me that he wouldn't make it." Sincere lowered his head as tears came to his eyes.

Vanessa was in awe. Usually it was the parent who gave up their dreams for the child's dream. "Do you regret it?" she asked softly.

"Actually, I'm a believer that everything happens for a reason. It's just life. So naturally, if I were to regret it, then I probably would've never met my wife who worked at the same nursing home where my dad was at."

"I'm a believer just like you. When I got into this business to help people, you'd be amazed at some of the stories I heard."

"More wine?"

"No, I shouldn't. It's getting late."
They had been talking for hours.

"Okay." Sincere looked slightly disappointed. He appeared to enjoy her company. He probably didn't realize how much talking about his feelings was a part of the healing process.

He made the first move. "Vanessa, can I see you again?"

Vanessa was at a loss for words.

"Can I?" He repeated the question while reaching for her hand.

An instant spark generated heat between them. She would be lying if she didn't admit that she was attracted to Sincere. There was something about him that drew her in.

She finally spoke up. "I don't think it's a good idea. I'm here to help you, and it just wouldn't be a good look—"

"Wait a minute," he stopped her. "I never agreed to anything. You may have come here to help me, but I didn't ask you to."

She gave him a side-eye.

"Don't get me wrong. I'm grateful, but this was all on you."

He was right. Vanessa had forced her way into his life. "Yes, we can see each other again."

He walked her to the door. "I had a great time tonight." Sincere pulled her into his arms and placed a light kiss on her closed lips. Holding her gently, he finally said, "I'll see you soon."

* * *

Sincere opened the door, and his eyes grew wide. "Ma? What are you doing here?"

Doreen stood there, visibly shaking, accompanied by an unknown visitor. Doreen couldn't speak.

"Hello, my name is—" the stranger said.

Doreen raised her hand. "No! I need to be the one to do this."

She gazed at Sincere. "Hi, Sin, can we come in? We need to talk. This is my friend Phyllis. She's my AA sponsor."

"Your what?" Sincere was at a loss for words.

Doreen lowered her head. "I can explain."

Vanessa started towards her car.

Sincere quickly reached for her. "Please don't go. I need you." He hoped she understood he needed her to stay.

He watched Doreen take a deep breath. *Is she really about to step inside?*

Phyllis was also watching her movements, and said, "It's okay. You can do it."

Doreen walked in slowly. As she looked around the room, she cried. They all took a seat in the living room and were quiet. No one knew what to say. Who would speak first?

After the long pause, Sincere spoke. "Ma, what happened to you once Dad passed?"

As the tears fell, she began to talk. "I remember when Sincere Sr. didn't want to buy this house. He said it had too many stairs. I convinced him anyway and eventually we were happy here. It wasn't until the day he got sick when things changed. He started to get worse, and I knew the end was near. Once he died, I picked up my first bottle right here in this room."

Sincere's eyes widened. He'd never known his mother to drink.

She looked around and began speaking again. "You were on the road, and I couldn't take being alone anymore. So, I drank a little at first and then as time went on, I drank a lot. By the time you came back home, I knew I had a problem."

Sincere knew the feeling when he thought about Tara. He lowered his head.

"That's when I realized I needed a fresh start, so I packed my belongings and left. I met Phyllis when I joined rehab. We shared a similar story, and she was able to help me get through it."

"Ma, why didn't you tell me?"

She shrugged. "You were so focused on running your father's business that I became invisible to you. I guess we were both hurting in our own way. But it's time for us to heal, Sin." Doreen glanced over at Vanessa who sat there quietly. "Don't you agree, Doctor?"

Vanessa nodded.

Doreen walked over to where Sincere was sitting and hugged him tight. They embraced while crying in each other's arms. Just what they needed.

"Are we okay?" Sincere asked, when they pulled apart.

Doreen smiled. "We will be. You're certainly in good hands." She winked at him. "I'm going to fly out tomorrow, but if you need anything, I'm here. Love you, Sin."

"Love you, too, Ma. Any chance you want to come back home?"

She smiled. "Believe it or not, I'm happy in New Jersey." They stood.

"Sincere, it's nice finally meeting you. Your mom has told me a lot about you," Phyllis said.

Sincere smiled. "Thank you, and please continue to look after her for me."

"Will do." Phyllis gave him a polite hug.

Doreen looked at Vanessa. "Dr. Stevens, before we leave, may I have a quick word with you. In private."

"Sure." Vanessa and Doreen stepped out the room.

"I just wanted to say thank you. I know when we first met, I probably made you nervous. But trust me, I scared myself. I'm also sorry I doubted you could help. However, I must say, I can tell Sincere's feeling better. Much more relaxed. He still needs time to heal, and I know you will respect that."

"Yes, ma'am. I will continue to be there for him."

"That's all I needed to hear." They shared a hug and returned to the others.

TRUE AFFECTION

Sincere and Vanessa spent a lot of time together over the next few months talking, going to lunch, dinner and the movies. She was falling for him. She tried to hold back, but couldn't help herself. Her feelings were becoming more real. They were returning to her office after having lunch at a nearby café. The light breeze made it a perfect day for a stroll as they held hands.

"What are you thinking about?" Vanessa asked.

"I'm thinking about how wonderful things have been between us." He stopped her from walking.

Vanessa felt his grip slip from hers. Her heart started to race. She had a feeling it wasn't the conversation she wanted to hear. He pulled her down to sit next to him on the bench outside her office building. Bracing for the worst, she nervously listened to him speak.

"Vanessa, thank you for bringing the sun back into my life during my darkest hour. The moment I felt everything slipping away from me, you helped give me the necessary air I needed to breathe. I'm thankful for a second chance to meet someone special, but I'm not sure if I'm ready to accept it. My brain tells me that I'm ready to move on, but my heart can't let go of the pain I still feel from losing Tara."

Vanessa frowned as she listened.

"I know we've been taking it slow and my feelings are growing for you more each day. But the conflict of opening up my heart to let you in has me thinking is it too soon?"

"I understand," Vanessa said with tears in her eyes. It wasn't every day that she fell head over heels for one of her clients. "Sincere, these past few months have been great! I never expected to get this close to you. And for that reason, I just want you to know that it's okay to let yourself be free. To accept that life goes on. Perhaps you might not find the soulmate you once had, but you can find love and companionship from someone who cares deeply for you. On that note, I better head back inside."

Before she let him see her cry, Vanessa stood, then turned and walked away.

* * *

The following week Vanessa threw herself into work. She hadn't heard from Sincere and missed him dearly. She was wrapping up with her latest client when her phone rang.

"Hello."

"Dr. Stevens?" the caller asked.

"Yes, how can I help you?"

"This is Patricia St. Jermaine. I barely recognized you. Why do you sound so down?"

"Hey, Professor Pat. I'm okay." She perked up. "This is a pleasant surprise. How's retirement treating you?"

Dr. St. Jermaine, affectionately known to her former students as Professor Pat, was a retired psychology professor from Stanford University. She'd taught alongside her husband, Scott, where they met years ago. They both shared common interests and had a love for teaching. The professor had told Vanessa there was always that one-star student she pushed harder than the others because she knew eventually, they would succeed. And it showed in Vanessa who came to the program with a full-ride academic scholarship for her tuition, room and board, textbooks, school materials and any other living costs, earning her PhD in psychology.

"How's your family? Professor Scott and your kids? You should be proud. I hear Derrick is the starting outside linebacker for the San Francisco Forty-Niners now."

"Yes, and my daughter, Sonya, is getting married soon."

"Wow, congratulations."

"Any new additions to the family?"

"No, no new grandbabies yet. Only Jayson, and he's spoiled rotten."

"So, how's business?" Patricia St. Jermaine asked.

"Business is good. Same old, same old..."

"Sounds like you're ready for a change. Are you open to hear about a new opportunity?"

"Sure." Vanessa listened intently and responded with a few words.

"You'll have your own rental space in my new commercial building, with connections to a major hospital in walking distance. I'll pay your relocation expenses to live in San Francisco. Your lease will be an affordable rate and includes your utilities and maintenance. How does that sound?"

How could she say no? This was a dream come true. Vanessa got excited until she thought about Sincere. She couldn't leave him, or could she?

"Thanks, Professor Pat, for the offer. I'm going to need a day or two to think about it."

Patricia St. Jermaine's silence said she was taken aback by her answer. This was a once-in-a-lifetime opportunity she was offering. "Alright, take the time you need. I'll talk to you soon."

"Okay. Thanks again. Bye."

MATTERS OF THE HEART

Vanessa made up her mind three days later. She accepted the offer to move to San Francisco, despite not hearing from Sincere. She owed it to herself to tell him about the great opportunity that had been presented to her. She scrolled through her phone to find his number.

* * *

Sincere was returning from an exhausting road trip. He thought about calling Vanessa, but decided against it. Instead of calling her, he pulled out his phone to check his voicemail. He had one new message.

"Hey, Sin, it's Mom. Just calling to check on you. Hope all is well. Give me a call when you get the chance. Love you."

Sincere was slightly disappointed after he heard the message, only to discover Vanessa hadn't called. *Should I call her? To say what?* he thought as he held the phone in his hand. Just when he was about to give up, his cell phone vibrated and Vanessa's name flashed across the screen. Perfect timing. He couldn't help but smile.

"Hello."

"Hey, Sincere." I know you're probably on the road, but I was hoping we could talk. I have something to tell you."

"Cool. I just got home and I have something to tell you, too, but rather than talk over the phone, why don't you come over in about an hour?"

"Sure, I can do that."

* * *

Sincere opened the door, genuinely happy to see Vanessa. She looked good in skinny jeans with a bright sweater and suede ankle boots. Her face was lightly made up, and her hair was pulled back. He reached out to hug her, and she hugged him back. In that moment, he realized how much he missed her. They broke apart from the embrace.

"It's good to see you," Sincere said.

"You too. How have you been?"

"Keeping busy..."

"Yeah, me too. Which is why I'm here."

"Okay, would you like something to drink?"

"No thanks, this won't take long. I just wanted you to know I was presented with a wonderful opportunity that I couldn't pass up."

"Really? What kind of opportunity?"

Vanessa filled him in on the details.

"Oh." Sincere was quiet, trying to mask his true feelings.

"What did you have to tell me?" she inquired.

"It wasn't that important." Sincere didn't reveal how he truly felt about her because he knew firsthand how it felt to have your dreams taken away. Even if it were of his own choosing. So, he wouldn't allow Vanessa to live with any regrets. As much as he wanted to beg her to stay, he wouldn't. No matter if it meant possibly losing her for good.

"Please don't go." He pulled her back into his arms, holding her close.

"I have to," Vanessa cried. "You live here in Atlanta, and I'm moving to San Francisco. There's too much distance between us that it simply won't work."

"Was this part of the plan? To bring new meaning back into my life so you could leave," Sincere said, visibly upset.

"Truthfully," Vanessa admitted, "I never expected to fall in love with you, but I did, and it cost me my heart." She stepped out of his embrace and looked at her Apple Watch for the time.

"What time is your flight?"

"In a couple of hours."

"Will I ever see you again?"

Vanessa shrugged. "I don't know... Goodbye, Sincere."

He watched her walk out the door on her way to the airport.

CAN'T HIDE LOVE

Present Day

"Wow! What a story. You said Sincere was not so sincere. I'm just trying to understand at what point in the story was that accurate." Lisa asked. "I get it, he's been through a lot, and while he was down, you helped lift him up. Which—don't get me wrong—was a part of your job. But falling in love with him? That's psychology rule number one: never get physically involved with your client."

Vanessa lowered her head. "I know, but I couldn't help it. Maybe it was him being

72

so loving when he spoke about his wife. The fact that you felt his raw emotions on how much he loved her."

Lisa scrunched up her face. "That sounds so creepy to me."

Vanessa rolled her eyes. "Not like that, Lisa. I'm just saying. We all want to be treated like a princess or at least feel like one. Well, with Sincere, he had that trait about him. Even after her death, his loyalty and the obvious guilt he felt. There didn't seem to be any doubts about who had his heart."

Vanessa shook her head. "What can I say? He stole my heart."

"Well, after the way you treated him earlier, it sounds like you want it back."

"What do you think I should do?"

"Wait. What?" Lisa put her hand on her chest. "Is the good doctor asking me for advice?"

"Stop playing. I'm serious," Vanessa whined.

"Well in that case, there's only one simple solution that I could think of."

"Yeah, and what's that?"

"Follow your heart..." Lisa said matter-of-factly, as she paid the check for them to leave.

* * *

Sincere blinked out of his trance as he sat there wrapping up his meal with Antonio.

"Everything alright, bro? You seem distracted."

That's an understatement, Sincere thought. "Hey, Antonio, can I ask for a favor?"

"Sure, what do you need?"

"Do you mind if I leave my truck here overnight? I thought I would get back on the road tonight, but I need to take care of some unfinished business."

"I'll tell you what. You can keep your truck here until Monday morning before the next schedule change. How does that sound?"

"Thanks, man. You think I can get a room too?"

Antonio glared at him. "Now you're pressing your luck. However, if you're paying, then I'll see what I can do."

"I owe you one."

"Okay, when you're ready, meet me at the front desk."

They patted each other on the back.

Sincere picked up Vanessa's business card and said aloud, "You're not getting away from me again this time." As he left the restaurant and got a room, he contemplated his next move.

Please Don't Go

Part Two

Part Two
Table of Contents

CARE FOR YOU

Sincere was at the Gwinnett Family Cemetery to visit Tara, his late wife's gravesite. He walked up to her headstone with a sad look on his face. No matter how long it had been since her death, it still wasn't any easier. He knelt and wiped away the scattered leaves and debris that had blown over top. He sat the bouquet of colorful daisies he was carrying next to her name. With tears in his eyes, he began to speak.

"Hey, Tara, my love. It's me. I miss you so much but I'm hanging in there. Things are different without you. The will to live. The dark moments I go through. Some

days I wish I could pick up the phone to hear your voice or walk in the house and see your smile. It's hard, T," he cried. "But I got some help to deal with the pain. I had to. And I know what you're thinking—why would I get a female therapist?" He envisioned her giving him the side-eye. "It wasn't my idea, babe, I swear. Although, I have to admit, I did enjoy having her around for a while until I pushed her away. What can I say? I felt guilty. Me and you never talked about seeing other people because we vowed to be together forever. Now, I'm lost without you." Sincere sat in silence for a while before saying, "Would it be okay if I continue to let Dr. Vanessa Stevens help me figure things out? That means I would have to pursue her. Trust me, she's not there to take your place. She's there to help soften the void of not having you around. I love you, Tara Lewis, always have, always will."

Sincere stirred himself awake and wondered why dreams often felt so real. He remembered the scene vividly, right before leaving Atlanta on his cross-country trip to San Francisco. He knew then he wanted to see Vanessa again. He just didn't know how until he ran into her the other day. What were the odds of that happening? *Was it Tara's way of giving her blessing?* Sincere had noticed the shock that registered across Vanessa's face when she recognized him. Her eyes were wide, filled with tears, hurt and pain as she looked up at him. Her voice was full of emotion when she angrily spat at him to *have a nice life* and walked away.

Snapping out of his thoughts, Sincere stepped out of bed and pulled the curtains back as the tenth-floor view from the Marriott Hotel was overcast by the morning fog. He stood there briefly and then walked over to the small wooden desk in the room.

80

Pulling out Vanessa's business card from his wallet, he studied the card for a moment, deep in thought. *What should I do?* he asked himself. Calling her would be the obvious choice, but Sincere knew it would take more than a phone call to get her attention. Finally, something came to mind. "That's it!" he said aloud, smiling at his sneaky plan. He quickly set her card on the desk and made his way to the bathroom to get cleaned up before heading out the door.

* * *

"Vanessa, you know what you need?" Lisa said, looking over at Vanessa who was sitting at her desk staring at nothing in particular. It was Sunday, and once again, they were back in the office because Vanessa insisted they had work to do.

"No, what's that?" Vanessa asked, blinking out of her trance.

"You need a vacation," Lisa replied. "You haven't been anywhere since I've known you."

"A vacation?" Vanessa sneered. "What's that? Have you forgotten I've been busy with running the company?"

"I get it. However, you can't keep burning yourself out like this. These clients...their problems... All I'm saying is you could use a break."

"A break, huh?" Vanessa thought about it. *Where would I go?* She hadn't traveled since leaving Atlanta over a year ago. She missed home. The hustle and bustle of the city known for its southern hospitality, diverse communities and award-winning restaurants. Traffic was a nightmare, but it was no different than San Francisco's in her eyes. No matter where you lived, you couldn't escape rush-hour traffic.

Truth be told, Vanessa also missed Sincere. However, since she hadn't heard from him, she figured he was long gone, back on the road by now. Who could blame him? After the way she treated him, she wouldn't have stuck around either. Although her heart was broken, it still wasn't the best way to handle the situation. *Maybe I should call him?* She quickly dismissed that idea. *He rejected you. Don't even think about it.*

"Thanks anyway, Lisa." She sighed. "I'm not going anywhere. I don't have the time."

Lisa shrugged. "Okay, it was just a suggestion." She turned back around to face her computer. They were both quiet for a while until the doorbell rang, breaking the silence in the room. They quickly looked at each other and wondered who could that be? It was outside of business hours.

Lisa became frightened and said, "Should we answer it?"

"Yes, it could be important."

"Okay, come with me."

"You're such a scaredy cat," Vanessa joked.

"No, I'm a safety cat. Whoever it is will have to grab the both of us."

They laughed while walking to the door.

* * *

Sincere stood in the doorway, holding his breath, when the sound of the lock turned, and Lisa opened the door with Vanessa closely behind her.

"Hello," Lisa greeted him with a polite smile. "This is a pleasant surprise, isn't it, Vanessa?"

Vanessa took a step forward. "Sincere, what are you doing here?"

He paused and blew out the air he'd been holding. "I was stopping by to leave something for you. But then, I noticed your car outside, so I took a chance to see if you were here. Do you have a moment?"

Vanessa stared at him for the longest time. So long, in fact, that Lisa cleared her throat to get her attention.

"Come on in," Vanessa slowly nodded and opened the door wider.

Sincere entered the building, and he immediately surveyed her office which was inviting and warm. The open floor space was simple, and the décor earth-toned colors. There was a small, glass modern style coffee table for beverages and tissues in front of a cozy sectional with fanciful pillows. Dr. Stevens' credentials hung on the wall along with affirmations and framed quotes from various motivational speakers. The surroundings created a peaceful environment.

"I'm really digging your office," he complimented her style.

"Thank you."

"Well, I'm going to head out, "Lisa said, breaking the awkward silence between them. She began to pack her things. "Sincere, it was nice seeing you again."

"Likewise."

"Vanessa, if you need anything, text me. And, remember what I said," she whispered close to her ear. "Follow your heart." She hugged her goodbye.

* * *

86

"Sincere, why are you here? I haven't seen you in a while, and we weren't exactly on speaking terms when I left." She offered him a seat on the sofa.

"I'm here because I was happy to see you the other day. I just thought..." Sincere stopped mid-sentence and sat down. Even though it was a serious conversation and he was ready to pour out his feelings, he still felt unsure of himself.

"Vanessa, I like you."

"You don't even know me."

"Well, give me a chance to get to know you."

"You had your chance and you blew it." She crossed her arms.

"That's not fair. You know I was going through a rough time. Let me make it up to you."

"How?"

"Come back to Atlanta with me."

Vanessa glared at him as if he had spoken a foreign language.

"I'm serious. We can do all the talking you want. We'll take our time on the drive. Do a little sightseeing. Try different foods. It'll be fun."

"Umm, sounds tempting," Vanessa confessed. She had never driven cross-country before. That was something on her bucket list of things to do. "How will I get back home?"

"Here. I came by to give you this." Sincere handed her the envelope he held in his hand.

Vanessa ripped it open and read the contents. "Wow! An open-ended plane ticket to Atlanta? For me? I don't understand."

"Yes. I was hoping you would use it one day to come visit me. I was going to leave it. With the note attached."

Vanessa smiled as she silently read his heartfelt letter of apology. "That was very thoughtful of you. Thank you."

"So, what do you say? You can fly back whenever you want." He could tell she was contemplating her answer. "I'll tell you what. I have to leave in the morning. So, why don't you take tonight to think about it?" He didn't want to push her into doing something she wasn't comfortable with.

Her heart fluttered at his words, and she grew excited about him wanting to see where things could lead. *"For once, do something out of the ordinary"* she could hear Lisa saying. No longer in doubt, she said, "Yes, I'll go with you."

"You will?" he said excitedly. Expecting her to say no.

"I said yes. Now let's get going before I change my mind." Vanessa cleared off her desk and then locked up her office. Sincere gave her some time to head home and pack for the road trip. They would meet at the Marriott Hotel.

SAY YES

The Marriott Union Square was a stylish, upscale hotel in a prime location close to downtown. It offered a ton of amenities, well-stocked bar, lounge area, and huge dining room with panoramic views of the city. Lisa walked into the restaurant and scanned it discreetly, as if she were meeting someone. She didn't have a reservation. However, she was determined to get the grilled salmon she'd been wanting to try. The lively hostess was just about to greet her when suddenly the gentleman standing there, whispered something, and then she quickly walked away.

"Hello, sorry for the interruption," he greeted Lisa with a smile. "I'm Antonio Matthews, general manager of the hotel." He extended his hand to hers. Lisa took in the sight of the handsome mixed-race guy with tan smooth skin, deep brown eyes and dark hair. He was tall, masculine and downright sexy with instant sex appeal, dressed in his designer suit and expensive shoes.

"Hi, I'm Lisa Pierce," she said as they exchanged handshakes. The electric shock that surged between their touch confirmed they were physically attracted to each other.

Playing it cool, Antonio said, "I remember you from the other night. You were here with your girlfriend, the one who was upset with Sincere."

"Oh yeah, sorry about that." Lisa's cheeks were flushed. "That was so embarrassing."

"No worries. Sincere is a good friend of mine. He explained that it was a misunderstanding between old friends. Apparently, they must have patched things up because your friend is waiting for him on the other side of the bar. I figured that's why you were here."

Lisa lifted a brow. "Actually, I came here to eat, but if you show me where she's seated…"

"Sure, you can follow me. Right this way." Antonio led the way.

Vanessa was sitting at the bar nursing a watered-down drink. An oversized Coach bag sat on the floor by her feet. She was casually dressed in a pair of bootcut jeans, cute top and denim jacket. Her shoulder length hair was tucked behind her ears to show off her pretty gold earrings.

"I'll give you two a minute and then I will show you to a table."

"Lisa watched him walk away. *Sheesh, that man is fine,* she mumbled to herself before returning her attention to Vanessa.

* * *

"Excuse me, is this seat taken?" Lisa asked in an unfamiliar tone.

Vanessa was focused on her iPhone. "No, help your–" she looked up and was surprised to see Lisa standing there.

"Hey, girl, what are you doing here? I was just texting you."

"Yeah, I hope it was juicy."

Vanessa grinned. "Better than juicy. I'm headed out of town with Sincere."

"Shut up! That must've been one hell of a talk. Where are you going?"

Vanessa filled her in on all the details.

"Now that's my idea of following your heart. I hope it works out for you."

"Me too." Vanessa was nervous. She wasn't one to throw caution to the wind. She was always careful. But in this case, she was willing to take the risk and leave with Sincere.

They stopped talking when they heard Sincere and Antonio approaching.

"You ready?" Sincere asked Vanessa.

"Yep, let's get this show on the road," she grabbed her bag.

"Sincere, now you already know...if anything happens, it's going to be me and you," Lisa warned.

"Don't worry, boss lady is in good hands with me."

"Okay, well you two be safe and call me when you get there."

Lisa and Vanessa hugged each other tight.

"Oh, and Lisa—"

Before Vanessa could say more, Lisa cut her off. "I know. Me and your *precious office* will be fine."

Antonio butted in, saying, "I'll make sure of it, Vanessa," he assured her and then he winked at Lisa. The two were all smiles as they waved goodbye to Vanessa and Sincere.

* * *

"Why don't you join me and my friends for dinner?" Antonio asked. "Once a week, we get together and talk about the latest current events." He could tell by her expression that Lisa was hesitant to accept his invitation.

"Please," he practically begged. "This way I don't have to be the third wheel watching them make mushy faces at each other all night long."

"Oh, your friends are in a relationship?"

"Yes, and sometimes they forget I'm there."

"Okay," she agreed, her voice soft, and she followed him to the table.

"Hey guys, sorry I'm late," Antonio greeted his friends. "I hope you don't mind, I brought a date. This is Lisa Pierce." They both smiled brightly.

"Lisa, these are my friends, Mike Edelin and his girlfriend, Megan Richards."

Lisa smiled. She recognized Megan from *Channel Five Sports Edition*. The TV personality looked exactly the same in person with her baby blue eyes, her blond flowing hair and perfectly shaped body that matched her gorgeous face. Mike was just as handsome and looked like a cover model with his milk chocolate skin, bald head and striking light brown eyes. They were a beautiful couple.

"About time," Megan blurted out. "Hi, Lisa, it's nice to meet you."

"Glad you could join us," said Mike.

After introductions were made, everyone settled into their seats.

"So how did you all meet?" Lisa was curious.

"Well," Antonio spoke first. "Mike and I are in the same industry. He's the general manager at Executive Inn and Suites in Oakland."

"Nice. I love that hotel," Lisa remarked.

"It's a beauty," Megan chimed in.

"So, we met at a hotel management training where we both got our start. We were sitting next to each other and were overwhelmed by the facilitator's presentation. We introduced ourselves and decided to compare notes. We instantly hit it off and as they say, the rest is history. I met Megan through Mike, although I was already a fan of her show."

"Cool, and what about you, Megan? How did you meet Mike?"

Mike and Megan looked at each other and laughed.

"To make a long story short," Megan said, "Mike almost got me killed."

"What?" Lisa's eyes widened.

"Okay, maybe not directly, but he was being blackmailed by someone that wanted me dead."

"That sounds awful."

"I didn't know it was a setup," Mike clarified.

"Wow! How did you overcome that?" Lisa wanted to know.

"Trust me, it involved a lot of talking to clear the air."

"And sex," Mike added.

Megan punched him in the arm. "What? Too much?"

Antonio and Lisa laughed.

"What about you two?" Megan asked, changing the subject.

"Actually, we just met tonight," Lisa replied.

"You did?" Megan raised a brow.

"My boy!" Mike high-fived him from across the table.

"Technically, I saw her the other day," Antonio retorted. "Her girlfriend was causing a scene with one of our suppliers."

Lisa rolled her eyes. "It was necessary."

"Really? I've never seen a therapist lose their cool and—."

"Wait? You're a therapist," Megan interrupted.

"My boss is. I'm a licensed case manager, but I assist her in certain areas."

As the night went on, the conversation flowed easily. They talked, laughed and reminisced. Everyone had a good time. In fact, Lisa and Megan exchanged numbers and agreed to meet for lunch soon. After saying their goodbyes, each couple went their separate ways.

Antonio and Lisa held hands as he walked her to her car.

"Thank you, Antonio. I had a great time."

"Me, too, and tomorrow I get you all to myself." He had set up the second date earlier.

"I'm looking forward to it." They stopped at her car. He held her gaze and lowered his head to kiss her. She gasped and he deepened the kiss, slowly, sliding his tongue inside her mouth. She automatically threw her arms around his neck. He could feel the heat of his desire gather within him. Headlights from a passing car caused them to reluctantly break apart.

"I better go," she said, as she reached for the door handle.

"Text me when you've made it home."

"I will. Have a good night, Antonio Matthews."

"Good night, Lisa Pierce."

DATE NIGHT

The next day Lisa was excited about her date with Antonio. It was almost time for him to pick her up from the office. He'd told her to dress for salsa dancing. *"On a Monday?"* she inquired while speaking to him over the phone. *"Yes,"* he told her. He wanted to see how well she moved her hips. Lucky for him, she was open to try it. Lisa wore a black form-fitting swing dress with three-inch Mary Jane heels. She added extra bounce to her natural curly hair and completed her look with light makeup. She knew enough to be cute but comfortable if they were going to be sweating. *Right on time*, she thought, as the doorbell rang.

"Hey, you." Lisa greeted Antonio when she opened the door.

"Hey, yourself." Antonio showed up wearing a long-sleeved button-down shirt, light-weight dress slacks and suede bottom shoes. He handed her a yellow long stem rose.

"Thank you." Lisa put it up to her nose and took a sniff of its aroma.

"You look great." He kissed her on the cheek. Are you ready to go?"

"I am." Lisa grabbed her sweater and clutch bag.

Twenty minutes later, they arrived and went inside SalsaCrazy Mondays at the Salsa Club on Clement Street. It was an ideal place to dance salsa, as well as other types of Latin dance, such as the bachata, the cha cha and the merengue. The space was large with plenty of room and a full bar. Antonio had a great passion for Latin dancing due to his mother's Hispanic heritage. They made their way onto the dance floor and the instructor taught them, along with other patrons, some basic moves. After a few practice steps, Lisa began to relax and enjoy herself. Salsa dancing wasn't so bad, after all.

"So, why are you single?" Antonio asked. They were taking a break and sat at a nearby table.

"I don't know." Lisa shrugged. "I guess I haven't found the 'one'."

"What do you consider 'the one'?"

"A lot of things. But to name a few... I have to be totally comfortable with him. He's supportive and happy to be around me. He shares some of the same values as me. For example, if I want kids, he should want them too. Basically, he loves me just the way I am."

"I hear you. I want the same things, too, but trust is high on my list. Being able to trust my partner is a must-have."

Out of the corner of her eye, Lisa saw something that spooked her. She immediately interrupted Antonio. "I'm sorry, Antonio, but I'm ready to go."

"Why?" he protested. "I thought we were having a great time."

"I know, but I have an early morning and need to get some rest."

"Are you okay?" He noticed the stress lines forming across her face.

"I'm fine. If you want to stay, I can take a Lyft."

Antonio looked at her as if to say, "you're kidding, right"? "No, I'll take you." They stood to leave. Antonio didn't know what caused her sudden mood change, as he followed her out the door.

* * *

The ride back to the office was quiet. Lisa had seemed distracted. Antonio double parked the car, and she quickly checked her surroundings before getting out.

"Thanks, Antonio, I enjoyed myself."

"I'm glad. When can I see you again?" He put his hands on her waist.

"I'll call you," she replied, giving him a quick kiss. She didn't linger this time like she had on their first date.

What just happened? he thought, as he watched her rush inside.

He was a little taken aback and didn't know what to think. He was confused because she wasn't talking. His imagination started to run wild. *Did I do something? Did I say the wrong thing?* He was determined to get to the bottom of it. Either way, he wasn't going to let it go, as he drove off.

ROAD TRIP

Days one and two of their trip Vanessa and Sincere drove non-stop through San Francisco, crossing over the Golden Gate Bridge and passing Bishop's Peak in San Luis Obispo. Pulling out her cell phone, Vanessa snapped a few pictures of the tallest volcanic mountains that were surrounded by trees, a mixed forest of oaks and bays. After driving long miles, they finally got out to stretch their legs and grab a bite to eat at the Grand Canyon National Park in Arizona. They admired the beauty that surrounded them: huge trees, rustic mountains and spectacular views. The area they traveled on, the *South*

Rim was definitely a picturesque masterpiece.

"This is so breathtaking," Vanessa said, enjoying the view. "I can't believe I've never been here before."

Sincere smiled. "I agree. People should experience this at least once."

Earlier, Sincere stopped by the local grocery store to pick up a bottle of sparkling wine and a simple pasta salad with chopped fresh vegetables and slices of grilled chicken. The weather was perfect, so he planned a makeshift picnic, with all the essentials, on one of the trails that overlooked the sunset.

"What are you thinking about?" Vanessa noticed him staring off into the distance.

"It's nice to be here with you," he said. "Thank you for accepting the invite. It's not easy for me to express myself, but I really want to explore whatever may happen between us. Is that possible? Will you be patient with me? I want to love again. Truthfully, I just don't know how."

Vanessa smiled. She wanted to be happy. To find someone that she could share her life with. She hadn't had much luck in the past. Somehow, she was always the one left with a broken heart. She knew had it not been for Sincere's wife passing, he wouldn't be here today. This time, she would give him the benefit of the doubt and take things slow.

"Sincere, I want to reconnect with you. That's one of the reasons why I'm here. I just hope you'll be able to open up to me."

"Come here," he said. Vanessa scooted between his legs and he covered her body from behind while pulling her close to him. There was something so peaceful about watching the sun go down over the hills. She didn't want the moment to end.

"I want to be open with you and going forward, I will try to be. I just need you to understand that I may not move at the pace you want me to, but if you give me a little time, I'll catch up. How does that sound?"

Vanessa smiled. At least he was willing to try, and that was more than she could ask for. "It sounds like you've got yourself a deal. So, where do we go from here?"

"Huh?"

Vanessa knew he wasn't following her.

"Babe, I just told you, I'm all in..."

She laughed. "Sweetie, I meant what is our next stop?"

"Oh." He joined her laughter. "When we leave here, we're headed to Albuquerque, New Mexico. We'll stay there overnight and then make our way to Texas."

"Dallas?" Her eyes lit up. She'd heard so much about the metropolitan area.

"Not quite, but we can stop wherever you want to go. It's just me, you and the open road. It's getting dark so we better start to head out. Plus, I need to refuel soon."

They both stood to leave. Vanessa started walking towards the truck. Sincere stopped her and pulled her into his arms. He wanted to kiss her. He could see the slight uncertainty as her eyes stared into his. It was up to him to make the first move. It had been a while since he touched her soft lips. With hearts beating wildly, he leaned forward and kissed her. He tightened his arms around her, and Vanessa grabbed his face. It was a tender kiss that left no room for misunderstanding. It was a lost connection that reignited a spark between them. As they continued their embrace, it was in that moment, he reaffirmed her place in his life.

* * *

112

Days three and four, one of the attractions that Vanessa wanted to visit in Dallas was the African American Museum. It was located in Fair Park, a small section in a residential town, so Sincere wouldn't be able to drive his truck there. He'd found a twenty-four-hour rest stop where he paid to park for a small fee. He planned for Uber to pick them up, and once they arrived at their destination, it was well worth it. The museum was huge. With several floors of various artwork lining the walls, gallery exhibits and a theater room that aired a short documentary on the African culture and its history. There was also a music section where you could view videos, and read about old and new performers. They spent half the day there before making their way to the gift shop. They each bought a few keepsake items and souvenirs to take home. Instead of eating at the museum, they walked nearby to Two Podners Restaurant, a nice, casual place with friendly waitstaff that served soul food. Vanessa ordered the pork rib tips, collard greens and mashed potatoes. Sincere settled on the oxtails over rice, sweet potatoes and cornbread. They washed it down with the sweet tea and lemonade mix known as an *Arnold Palmer*.

* * *

"That was an amazing experience," Vanessa said, referring to their earlier visit to the museum. "Although it was out of the way, I'm glad we went." They were back in the truck, on the road headed to Memphis. She stifled a yawn. She was exhausted. The long hours in an eighteen-wheeler were finally catching up with her.

"How do you do it?" she asked. "This job would drive me crazy."

Sincere smiled. "It has its moments, but you get used to it. When my dad got sick, I stepped in to take over the business. At first, I didn't think I could do it. I kept stopping and taking breaks because it got boring. Then, one day, I came home ready to give up. I remember my dad saying, 'Son, this is a business. You have to treat it as such. A delivery driver doesn't get paid if he's not delivering.'"

"Wise words."

"True and that's when I became addicted to caffeine and energy drinks. Don't laugh."

She covered her mouth.

"I had to...in order to test my skills and see if I preferred driving early mornings or late at night. Believe it or not, there are perks that come with this lifestyle."

"Oh yeah, like what?"

"Like—the great food we just ate. The unique views of various states. I can play my music as loud as I want. I'm the boss, so I set my own schedule. Not to mention, I can dress however I want."

Vanessa glanced at his athletic figure, short-cropped wavy hair, dark eyes and his boyish good looks. His large, well-defined muscles were revealed in the short-sleeve shirt he wore paired with carpenter jeans and work boots.

"I see. You're a real looker," she teased.

"Oh, it's like that," he snapped back. "Don't get it twisted, I can certainly rock an Armani suit, Gucci shoes and Rolex watch." They laughed and then rode a while in comfortable silence.

Vanessa had dozed off. Sincere wanted to keep going, but his eyes were fighting to

116

stay open. Normally, when that happened, he would pull over on the side of the road and take a nap. However, Vanessa was with him, so he drove to the nearest rest stop.

* * *

Days five and six were the last leg of their trip when they had arrived in Downtown Memphis. Beale Street which runs from the Mississippi River to East Street catered to locals and tourists who strolled the city's blocks. There was plenty of entertainment from restaurants, shops and nightclubs. It was also home to some of the best music, featuring blues, rock 'n' roll and R&B. Once again, Sincere found a place to park his truck. Neither one of them were heavy drinkers, so they wandered the streets ending up at the iconic B.B. King Blues Club to check out a live band. The atmosphere was nice but Vanessa wasn't all that impressed.

"Are you ready to go?" Sincere asked, noticing her obvious fatigue.

"Yes, and please tell me the next stop is home," she confirmed his suspicions.

"Alright, if we leave now, we'll be in Atlanta in no time." They made their way to the exit.

A few hours later, they pulled up to Sincere's trucking company to store his truck. He turned off security and unlocked the gate. Once he was done, he reset the alarm and they hopped in his SUV.

"Do you need anything before we head in?" he asked.

"No, I'm fine."

"Okay, I figured we could have breakfast in the morning."

"Sounds good."

Vanessa and Sincere entered his three-bedroom home in Snellville. Just as she remembered, the hardwood floors led directly into a spacious kitchen with granite countertops, cherrywood cabinets and stainless-steel appliances. The two-story structure also had two and half baths, a large living room, family room and master bedroom.

"You can stay and freshen up in the upstairs guestroom. There are some clean towels in the linen closet behind the door. It's been a long six days, so I'll let you get some rest."

"Thanks, Sincere, for everything. I had a wonderful time," she said, visibly tired.

He leaned in and kissed her on the lips. He pulled her close in an embrace. Finally, he pulled away and turned to walk off. She stopped him.

"Please don't go. Will you stay with me?" She gazed into his eyes.

Without hesitation, he said, "I want you."

She hadn't said a word, but the sexual desire longing within them could be felt. The overwhelming urge to touch one another. He lifted her off her feet and carried her to the bed in the room. He laid her down and rested his large body on top of hers. Their lips connected in a deep intimate kiss.

She moaned, as Sincere's hands started to wander over her body. They were making out, breathing heavily, and Vanessa pulled apart from him only for a moment to say, "I want you too." Nothing else was said between them, as they slowly got undressed and became one with each other's bodies.

LIVE IN THE MOMENT

The next morning Vanessa and Sincere woke up in each other's arms. The sun peeking through the blinds. "Good morning, beautiful," he said, placing light kisses on her back. "How'd you sleep?"

"Like a baby," she snuggled up against him, feeling his penis, hard and ready.

"Are you hungry?" he asked.

"Yes, but it can wait," she stroked Sincere briefly, before guiding him into her from behind.

"Ahh," she cried when he thrust into her. It had been a while for him, so last night's lovemaking was brief. Not to mention, they were both exhausted from the trip.

However, this morning he was penetrating into her hard and going deep.

"You feel so good." He thrusted in and out of her. Her orgasm was building, her body tingled from head to toe as she lifted her hips and arched her back. His hands cupped her breasts and he pushed into her one last time before pulling out and releasing himself. Sincere fell onto his back. "That was incredible! I want to hold you all day." He shifted to one side and drew her close. She reached up and pulled the blanket and wrapped it around them. She snuggled her face into his neck.

"Sincere..."

"Shh, don't say anything. Let me have this moment." He knew she wanted to talk about something more serious. Most likely, the dreaded conversation of where did they go from here? Honestly, he didn't know what was on her mind. He knew she had to go home sooner or later. For now, he stroked her back as they lay in comfortable silence.

* * *

A few hours later, Vanessa and Sincere finally got out of bed after another round of lovemaking and falling back to sleep. They showered, dressed and headed out to get something to eat. Once they ate, they were taking a stroll through his neighborhood before stopping at a nearby park.

"Sincere..." Vanessa stopped walking as she pulled him down to sit next to her on an empty bench.

He immediately felt a sense of déjà vu. "What's on your mind?" he asked. By her expression, he could tell it wasn't the conversation he wanted to hear.

She linked her hand into his as she nervously began to speak. "I'm thinking about how this has been a wonderful week. Spending time with you. Getting to know you. You getting to know me. This is what I was hoping for. Dreaming of. The moment you opened up to me. The way you were so gentle when our bodies first touched. I know you're the *one* for me. And that's why...this is so hard, because I don't know how I'm going to be able to leave you. How do I let you go?" Vanessa started to cry.

Sincere pulled her close. "Vanessa, I'm sorry, this is my fault. I was being selfish and really didn't think this thing out. I just knew I wanted you here with me, and for some strange reason, I thought once we were together, you would stay. I'm falling for you, but I understand that you have your life in San Francisco and I have mine here in Atlanta. I can't expect you to walk away from it all... But, could you?"

"I could ask you the same question. Could you?"

They challenged each other. Neither said a word.

"On that note, I guess we better head back inside," Sincere said as he stood and pulled her to her feet. He embraced her. Clearly, they were at a crossroads on which path they would take. Would she move? Would he move? Or would they make a long-distance relationship work? Only time would tell.

STAY ALERT

By the end of the week, Lisa and Megan were out having brunch at Bistro Central Parc, a cozy, hidden gem near McAllister Street that served French cuisine.

"Have you talked to Antonio?" Megan asked while forking a bite of salad into her mouth.

"Briefly, I've been avoiding him."

"Why? I thought you two were feeling each other."

"I am. I do like him. It's just that...you ever get the feeling that you're being watched?"

Megan could relate as she thought back to when she was being followed in

126

Miami by someone unknown. Until she found out it was Officer Williams. Officer Williams was seeking revenge on Megan because she was still bitter at her for having an affair with her late husband. Surprisingly, their beef was resolved when Officer Williams was the responding officer who helped save Megan from being killed.

"Well, take it from me, trust no one. I mean, don't get me wrong, I love Antonio like a brother but anything's possible." Lisa's case was a little different than Megan's because she pretty much knew who it was. She just didn't know what the person was capable of, so she kept her distance from Antonio.

"Excuse me... Megan Richards, is that you?"

Megan looked up and smiled. Lisa nearly froze in her seat, terrified as she stared at her former boss, Sarah.

"Oh my God, I'm such a fan of the show," she said in a high-pitched tone. "Do you mind if we take a selfie?"

"No, not at all." Megan was clueless.

"Thank you. You two ladies have a nice day." Sarah winked at Lisa and then she quickly moved on. Sarah couldn't seem to help herself; she was attracted to Lisa. She hadn't expected her to quit her job, and when she did, she became obsessed with wanting to see her again.

Lisa cringed and whispered over the table. "That's her."

"That's who?" Megan looked around the room.

Lisa shook her head. "My former boss."

"Really? The girl next door chick—"

"Girl next door my ass... she's super aggressive."

"Well then, don't wait. Get a temporary restraining order."

That's easier said than done, Lisa thought. If she didn't report her sexual advances to HR when she worked with her, why would she go to the police? Besides, she hadn't really done anything but follow her around to a few places.

"I'm telling you, people like that don't take no for an answer until someone gets hurt." Lisa had a worried look on her face.

"Don't worry, I've got your back." Unbeknownst to Lisa, Megan had already texted Mike and Antonio and told them what was going on. She wasn't taking any chances. The operation to take down Sarah was in full effect.

* * *

Lisa, Antonio, Megan and Mike were all meeting at the Marriott for their usual once a week gathering to devise a plan on how to take down Sarah.

"I know how we can get rid of her?" Antonio said.

"How?" Lisa wanted to know. After explaining the situation to him, Antonio refused to keep his distance from her. If anything, he felt she needed him now more than ever.

"We give her a taste of her own medicine. We start to make her feel uncomfortable. It won't be fun and games anymore when she's the one looking over her shoulders."

Mike interrupted and said, "That actually makes sense to me and I know someone who could help."

Antonio continued, "See, when you didn't report Sarah and let her get away with her inappropriate behavior, you gave her the upper hand. So, now she's messing with your mind."

"What do you think I should do?" Lisa asked Antonio.

"You mean, what are *we* going to do?" Antonio assured her. Megan and Mike agreed.

Lisa smiled. Although, she hadn't known them long, it felt good to have their support.

"Don't look now, but here she comes." Antonio spotted Sarah from across the room. "Okay, Megan, you're up. You remember what to do?"

"I got it." Megan rose from her seat and made her way over to Sarah.

"Hey look everyone, it's my friend, Sarah," she said loudly. "It's so good to see you again." Megan pulled out her phone. "Let's take another selfie."

Sarah's face turned bright red. She wasn't expecting the unwanted attention. She tried to pull away, but Megan snapped the picture anyway. "Where you going? Don't run off. Bartender, can you get her a drink?"

"Sure." The bartender walked over to their table.

"No, that's okay. I have to get going." She waved him off.

It was Antonio's turn to step in. "Is everything alright? I'm the manager of the hotel. Can I help you with something, Ms.?" He then looked over at Megan. "Ms. Richards, please don't harass the guest."

Sarah said, "She's fine. I just need valet to get my car."

"No problem, I can take care of that for you." Antonio took her ticket. "Here you go, license plate, PDGTL3. We have you on file, Sarah Marie Grace."

Megan lowered her voice. "When you mess with Lisa, you mess with us."

"Stay away from her," Antonio warned, handing her back the ticket.

Again, Sarah tried to run off and that's when she bumped into Mike who was talking to Officer Williams. After Megan's incident, Officer Williams transferred from Oakland's police department and went back to being a city cop at SFPD. She was on duty in the area and stopped by the hotel in full uniform.

"Officer Williams, this is Sarah, the girl I was telling you about," Mike said.

Officer Williams could tell she got the point when her eyes widened. "Hello," she said, "If you don't want to see me again, I suggest you leave these fine people alone."

Sarah didn't say a word and rushed out the door.

ALL I NEED

After Lisa thanked everyone for helping her out, she and Antonio were having a private dinner in the Junior Suite on the twenty-sixth floor. The room was spacious and bright. It included a separate bedroom with a king bed. Granite and tiled bathroom with rainfall shower and tub. A large living room and beautiful city views. Being the general manager, this was one of the employee perks he hadn't taken advantage of until now.

"This is amazing," she said, admiring her surroundings.

"You're amazing." He walked up behind her, placing his arms around her waist. He tightened his grip and whispered, "Make love to me."

Lisa melted into his arms as he pressed light kisses on her neck. Unable to resist, she turned to face him. "Do you think Sarah will continue to follow me?"

He shrugged. "Who knows what stalkers do? I just know we won't let her get away with it."

Lisa was quiet.

"Baby, come here." He took her by the hand and led her to the next room where they sat on the bed.

"Tell me, what's on your mind?"

"I don't know. Megan said something earlier that bothered me."

"Like what?"

"She said people like Sarah won't give up until someone gets hurt. So that still makes me a little nervous."

Antonio felt helpless. He knew there was a chance of them seeing Sarah again. It was just a matter of time. For now, he wanted to assure her that as long as he was around, she would have nothing to worry about.

"I won't let anything happen to you."

"You promise?" she said with the saddest puppy dog eyes.

"I promise. If you keep me close." Antonio scooted closer and wrapped his arms around her. He pressed a gentle kiss to her lips. What was intended to chase away her fears quickly ignited a deeper exchange when she crushed her body tighter against him and opened her mouth for his exploring tongue.

Fully aroused, he eased her back on the bed, while she pulled him forward to cover her. His erection pressing on her stomach signaled his urgent need for her matched the need she was projecting for him.

Reaching up to caress his face, she said, "Make love to me now. Please." When she reached for the zipper to pull off her dress, Antonio grabbed her hand and kissed the palm.

Gazing into her eyes, he said, "Oh no, babe. You know I've been watching this zipper all night and wondering if I would get a chance to unwrap all this lusciousness. And now the pleasure is all mine."

Lisa had seen the sexy denim creation in a boutique display window and after trying it on, the salesclerk had predicted she wouldn't be wearing it long around the right man. The woman had even tissue-wrapped a scandalous bra and thong set—that made Lisa blush—in the bag. The dress, a simple mid-thigh number sported a long gold zipper that extended from her enticing cleavage to a slit a few inches from the short hem. Clinging to all her curves, it proved the boutique clerk right. At first sight, Antonio froze and dropped the single yellow long stemmed rose he'd begun to bring her every time he saw her. Appearing hypnotized, he'd barely taken his eyes off her all evening.

Grasping the heart-shaped zipper pull between his fingers, he slowly kissed and nipped her exposed skin until her dress parted all the way open. He removed the dress and made quick work of unclasping her wispy lace bra, and ripping away the matching soaked thong, bringing it to his nose before stuffing it in his back pocket.

Overwhelmed by the vision in front of him, he whispered, "You are beautiful, gorgeous woman, and I'm glad you're mine.

Lisa moaned as he caressed and gently squeezed her breasts before taking her brown nipples into his mouth. He sucked and nibbled, moving from one stiff nipple to the other. She arched her back and held his head tighter to her breast. One of his hands traveled down her stomach to explore the feminine mound between her legs. She lifted and twisted her hips to grind against his hand as he stroked and teased her clit. "Baby, you are so wet for me, and I have to taste you."

He pressed kisses between her legs, wrapping his arms around her thighs and spreading her open to receive his lips and tongue while sucking her clit.

The intoxicating scent from her desire was driving him crazy, and he didn't know how much longer he could contain himself. But he needed to satisfy her first.

He felt her body trembling and tasted her juices flowing as her whimpers and incoherent pleas grew louder. Her screams rose as her body stiffened and an orgasm rendered her helpless.

So aroused and weakened himself, he stood and quickly stripped off his clothes and rolled on the condom he'd removed from his pants pocket, all the while watching her glazed eyes as she attempted to bring her breathing under control. Her outstretched arms welcomed him into a warm embrace and he joined her on the king-sized bed.

He wanted her and he wanted her now. The electric charge he felt from their naked bodies touching had him gripping her hips to hold her close as he thrust deeply into her, joining their bodies together for the first time. Antonio was falling for Lisa Pierce and never imagined being inside the woman would bring him so much pleasure. With each thrust, her passionate response was driving him out of his mind.

* * *

Lisa was still half asleep as she glanced over at a sleeping Antonio when her cell phone rang. "Hello," she whispered into the phone. She sat up, looked around for her dress and climbed out of bed. Pulling it on, she went into the bathroom and closed the door.

"Hi Lisa, how are you?" Vanessa said into the phone.

"Hey, I'm good. How are you? How's your trip?"

"Trip is great, I'm having so much fun! We've been so many places. America is truly diverse, with various pop cultures. It's been an awesome experience and Sincere's been...." Vanessa paused and held the phone.

"Let me guess," Lisa teased, "very sincere."

"He's been all that I dreamed he would be. And more. Lisa, he's wonderful!"

"Sounds like you two had sex." Lisa could tell by the giddy tone in her voice.

"Girl, yes!" Vanessa said. "Over and over and over…"

"Okay, I get it." Lisa stopped her. "The sex is great!" She was happy for Vanessa. She deserved to find love, but there was a problem. How was she going to keep it?

"So, are you going to stay with him a little while longer?" Lisa inquired.

"Unfortunately, it has to end soon."

"Why does it have to end?"

"You know why? I have to come back home. I can't stay here forever. I have a business to run. Clients to see. Speaking of which, how are my clients?"

"All is well. You know there's always that one though, that misses you like crazy. But for the most part, it's been quiet."

"That's good, and what about you? Are you behaving yourself or are you playing? I saw how Antonio was checking you out before we left."

Lisa blushed. "Ummm, let's just say, we're having a great time getting to know each other. I'll fill you in on everything when you get back. In the meantime, do you want me to book your flight?"

"No, I'll take care of it."

"Okay then, thanks for calling. And keep me posted."

* * *

It was the day of Vanessa's departure and Sincere had driven her to the airport. She wasn't ready to leave, but she couldn't stay either. Back in the real world, she had responsibilities, and owning her own practice was a dream come true. A moment she had worked so hard to achieve. She was happy and didn't have any regrets with the decisions she'd made. Being in a committed relationship was important to her, however, how long would that last when they lived in different states?

Sincere was having those same exact thoughts. Atlanta was his home where he was born and raised. With so many treasured memories, the highs and lows as well as the emotional journey to get to where he was. How could he leave it all behind?

Vanessa's tears were impossible to hold back as they rushed down her face. Saying goodbye was a whole lot harder than she'd imagined. Especially this time around since they had gotten closer. She hugged him tight before heading towards airport security.

"Please don't go," he whispered in her ear.

"I have to," she cried, "but I'll come back to visit you."

"When?"

"I'll call you" was all she could say.

In that moment, she wished she could've said, "to hell with it, I'll stay." They kissed and hugged each other dearly until it was time for her to go. She stepped out of his embrace, waved goodbye, and slowly walked away.

Sincere didn't move. He stood there with tears in his eyes and watched her disappear from his sight. What was he going to do now? Would he go after her or get over it? He looked at the time. If he wanted to catch her flight, a decision needed to be made soon. He began to wander off and pondered on which direction he was headed.

Please Don't Go

Part Three

Part Three
Table of Contents

HIDE AND SEEK

Sincere sat in the airport terminal for what felt like hours. As much as he wanted to get on the plane and go after Vanessa, he knew it wouldn't prove anything. He wasn't ready to move from Atlanta any more than she was willing to leave San Francisco. But who was he fooling? He missed Vanessa already, and it hadn't even been twenty-four hours. Snapping out of his thoughts, he finally made a decision. Sincere pulled out his cell phone to make a call. He needed some advice and knew just where to get it from.

"Hello."

"Hi, Ma," Sincere said when his mother, Doreen Lewis, answered the phone.

"Hey, Sincere." She was happy to hear from him. Call it a mother's intuition, but she could tell something was wrong by the tone of his voice.

"Are you okay, son?"

"I'm fine. Can I come see you?"

Doreen paused, surprised by his unexpected question. A while ago, he'd made it clear that he wasn't interested in visiting her if she couldn't visit him. Since then, she had already faced her fears and went to visit him. So, she wondered, what could this be about?

"Sure. Of course, you can. When should I expect you?"

"In a few hours."

"Okay. See you soon."

Sincere ended the call and walked over to Delta Air Lines. Instead of heading home to an empty house with a feeling of regret. He booked a round-trip ticket to New Jersey to spend time with his mom.

* * *

Meanwhile, Lisa was parked at the San Francisco airport waiting to pick up Vanessa who was returning home from her trip to Atlanta. Lisa hugged her as soon as she walked out.

"Hey, Vanessa. Welcome back, you look—" Lisa stopped mid-sentence and studied her face. She wanted to say relaxed, but there was a slight sadness in her eyes. "Why do you look so down? I thought you had a great time. Lisa placed her luggage in the car.

"I had a wonderful time. I just hate that it had to end, that's all." They got into the car.

"How are you?" Vanessa asked. "You're looking all cute." She admired her wild natural curly hair, ripped blue jeans, bell-sleeved top and the long vest that layered her outfit.

"Thank you." Lisa's skin was glowing.

"What did I miss?" Vanessa wanted to know.

"Well for starters, I'm dating Antonio, and things are going great!"

"I'm not surprised," Vanessa said. "I knew there was something going on because you two couldn't stop smiling at each other. He seems like a nice guy."

"Yes, he is." Lisa got quiet.

"Ut oh, what's the matter? Or should I say, what's not perfect about him?" Vanessa joked.

Lisa shook her head. "This isn't about Antonio...there was a slight problem while you were away."

"Really, what happened?" Vanessa asked concerned.

"It's about Sarah."

"Sarah?" Vanessa repeated. Then it came to her. "Oh, Sarah as in your former boss? What did she do?"

"It's kind of creepy. She's been following me around lately."

"What? Are you serious? Is she stalking you?"

"Yes, I think so. She pops up everywhere I go."

"Oh my God! That's scary. Why didn't you tell me?"

"I don't know." Lisa shrugged. "At first I thought it was a coincidence until she was confronted about it."

"I assume you went to the police."

"Not exactly. Antonio and his friends scared her off."

Vanessa raised a brow. "I find that hard to believe."

"Me, too. Which brings me to my next question. Do you think we should get a security system at the office?"

Vanessa thought about it; although she felt like they were in a safe neighborhood, you couldn't be too sure nowadays. "That may not be a bad idea."

Lisa was relieved. "Okay, I'll call a few companies in the area and get some quotes. Thanks, Vanessa, for understanding. I'm glad you're back."

They rode in silence for the rest of the way home.

* * *

Sincere followed the GPS directions from Newark airport and took Route One South to his destination. Twenty minutes later, he parked the rental car in front of his mother's complex, Park Place Townhouses, located in Avenel, New Jersey. A pleasant suburb with a lot of restaurants, coffee shops and community parks. An area accessible to all the major highways and two huge shopping malls nearby. His mother opened the door to her unit and greeted him with a tight hug.

"Hey, Sin. It's so good to see you. Come on in."

"Thanks, Ma, for having me. I know it was short notice, but I needed to get away for a bit to clear my head..."

Doreen waved him off. "You are more than welcome here anytime. You know that. Let me show you around."

She led him into her spacious two-story, two-bedroom home with two and half baths, formal dining area, wood burning fireplace in the living room, kitchen, and a small patio. The upper level housed the spare bedroom, full bath and master suite with a walk-in closet.

"This is perfect for you, Ma. I see why you didn't want to come back to Atlanta," he joked.

Sincere set his overnight bag down on the bed in the guest room and followed her back downstairs.

"Are you hungry?" she asked, while walking into the kitchen. "I just finished making one of your favorite meals."

His eyes lit up. "You made lasagna?"

"Yep, I sure did," she exclaimed. "Now go wash your hands and then let's eat," she said, pointing him to the powder room in the hallway.

* * *

Doreen blessed the food and she and Sincere began eating. After a few bites, his mother asked, "How are you and Vanessa doing?"

Sincere smiled. Although he couldn't stop thinking about her, he had mixed emotions. On one hand, he enjoyed being with her, but on the other, he still felt guilty. Like he shouldn't be moving on so soon after Tara's death.

"Ma, how come you never dated anyone after Dad's death?"

Doreen's facial expression changed. She stopped eating and her gaze wandered over his curious face. She shrugged as she slowly replied, "Your dad was my everything. We were childhood sweethearts. My first love. When he died, it wasn't easy for me. So, the last thing on my mind was finding someone new. Besides, at this stage in my life, I'm content with the memories we shared..." She blinked back tears.

"Don't you get lonely sometimes?"

"Sure, I do, but I have other things to keep me busy. Sincere, I know what this is about." She could see the agony on his face, that he was still struggling with Tara's death. "You know I loved Tara like a daughter. She was a beautiful spirit. A kind-hearted individual who always wore a smile."

Tears formed in Sincere's eyes.

"You two were happy, and I'm sure you planned to spend the rest of your lives together. But God had other plans. And I'm not saying you have to forget about Tara, but you're young, son. It's okay to let go of the pain, rebuild your life and have fun."

"I'm trying, Ma, but it's hard. I just want things to go back to the way they were. I miss Tara so much," he cried.

"I know you do." Doreen got up from her seat and knelt by his side to comfort him. Her heart broke for her son. Sincere was always strong and kept to himself, so this conversation between them was long overdue. He sobbed uncontrollably for a while, and then his mother softly said, "I think you should sell the house."

Sincere wiped his eyes and blew his nose. He shook his head. "Ma, I can't leave Atlanta."

"Who said anything about leaving?"

"Well, you're asking me to sell the house. I'm confused."

"Yes, because if you don't, you're going to push Vanessa away."

158

"What do you mean by that?"

Doreen rose to her feet and returned to her seat at the table. "Listen to me. That house is older than you with a ton of memories."

"I know, so why would I—"

"That's just it, Sin. They're your memories, not Vanessa's. Although, she's a doctor and it's her job to relate and understand what you're going through. But when it comes to her personal life, trust and believe, she won't live in the shadows of your deceased wife."

Sincere didn't say a word. He knew there was truth in his mother's words. His phone buzzed, and it was a text from Vanessa letting him know she had made it home safely. He quickly texted her back and then returned to talking with his mother.

"Thanks, Ma, I think I know what I need to do."

"I'm glad you're feeling better. Are you leaving now?"

Sincere laughed. "No, I need another home-cooked meal before I go."

"Okay great. Tomorrow I'll take you to my favorite grocery store. It's called Shoprite and you'll love it there."

Sincere helped his mom clean up the kitchen and then headed up to his room for the night. It had been a long day, but he wanted to call Vanessa before he went to sleep.

* * *

There was a three-hour time difference when Sincere pulled out his cell phone. It was close to midnight where he was and just before nine o'clock on the west coast. After the long talk with his mother, he wanted to hear Vanessa's voice.

160

"Hello."

"Hi, sweetie." Noticing the time, she asked him, "What are you still doing up?"

"Thinking about you. I miss you," he said above a whisper.

Vanessa smiled. "I miss you too. I can't wait to see you again."

"Earlier, I was so close to getting on the plane and following you back home," he admitted.

"Really? Why didn't you?"

"I don't know," he said truthfully. "I came to see my mom instead."

"Oh, you're in New Jersey?"

"Yes."

"Nice. Tell your mom I said hello."

"Will do. Vanessa...?" He paused as if to choose his words carefully.

"Yes," she quickly responded. Her heart thumped against her chest, anticipating his next words.

"I'll be back to see you soon. Have a good night."

"I hope so, Sincere. Goodnight," she said, and hung up the phone.

SAFETY FIRST

The next morning, Keith Knight rang the bell to the office of his next appointment. After several minutes, two beautiful African American women came to the door. They checked his credentials before allowing him to come inside. *That was a smart thing to do,* he thought. But with certain security measures in place, the awkwardness could've been avoided.

"Hello, ladies. I'm Keith Knight from Knight and Day Security Systems. Someone called for a consultation."

"That would be me." Lisa stepped forward. After the incident with Sarah, it was time to tighten up on security around the office. She came across his website while searching Google. His company was a small black-owned business specializing in the installation of alarm systems that were configured, installed, dismantled and programmed. Keith was not only the owner, but he was also the lead installer for his commercial and residential customers. Never the average sit-behind-the-desk type of guy, he enjoyed the responsibilities of getting his hands dirty from running wires under carpets, drilling holes in walls to enter crawl spaces when necessary. At thirty-six, five-eleven, smooth chocolate skin, he was physically strong with an athletic frame. He wore a blue polo shirt with his company logo on the front, khaki pants and plain canvas shoes.

Keith scanned the room, making a mental note on where cameras could be added. He tried his best to remain professional, however, he couldn't help but notice how beautiful Vanessa was. Tall, slender with dark brown skin and jet-black hair. She looked straight at him with her piercing brown eyes. Thinking she was the one worried about her safety, he assured her, "I'll make sure you have all the necessary equipment you need."

"Thanks, but I'm not—"

Lisa touched Vanessa's arm to stop her from speaking. "We'll appreciate anything you can do for us," she butted in, after noticing the subtle attraction Keith had for Vanessa.

"When can you start?" Lisa asked.

"When do you need me to start? Installation takes about a half a day, depending on how many cameras you're ordering. Look, here's my card." He handed it to Vanessa, although Lisa was the one doing the talking. "Think about it and give me a call when you're ready."

Keith focused his attention back on business and said, "Keep in mind that the longer you wait, the more at risk you are for a possible threat to happen."

"Thank you for stopping by." Lisa smiled. "I'll be in touch to set up a date and time as she walked him to the door.

* * *

Two days later, Vanessa and Lisa settled on getting one camera at the entrance with a silent alarm feature that would be monitored by the local authorities. This way they could keep track of who was entering and leaving the premises.

"You're all set, ladies." Keith had finished installing and programming the new system. It was an easy job, but he took his time giving them step-by-step instructions on how it works. "Do you have any questions?"

Vanessa and Lisa looked at each other. They both shook their heads *no*.

"Okay then, I guess I'll be on my way." He bent down to pick up his work bag.

Vanessa stopped him. "Do you have a minute?" she inquired.

"Me?" Keith pointed to himself as he looked at her, confused. "Sure." He nodded.

"This won't take long," Vanessa assured him and led the way into her office.

Lisa went to her desk while Vanessa closed the door behind them and offered him a seat.

"Is everything alright?" he asked, concerned. Vanessa hadn't said two words to him since he had been there. Earlier, he tried to make small talk with her, but nothing was said. Not even a glance his way. He got the hint and continued to work in silence.

"I brought you in here to apologize for my behavior," Vanessa said, genuine regret in her voice. She was normally polite. However, ever since she and Sincere parted, her attitude had changed; she was a bit moodier.

"It was uncalled for," she admitted, "but I truly appreciate all that you've done to make our office feel secure."

Keith sympathized. "I understand. If I felt threatened by someone, I would probably be on high alert myself." He thought that was the reason for her agitation. Vanessa didn't deny or confirm his suspicions. He moved on. "I was wondering if we could...." he was interrupted by her ringing phone.

"One second please," she held up a finger to answer the internal call. "Yes Lisa?"

She listened intently. "Okay, tell them I'll be there shortly." She hung up.

"I'm sorry about that. I'm needed over at Kaiser. What were you saying?"

"I was wondering if we could go out sometime?"

Caught off guard by his question, Vanessa was speechless. Before she could turn him down, he stood and gazed so deeply at her, it was at that moment when she felt his vibe.

"Think about it and I'll be in touch soon," he said on his way out the door.

LETTING GO

Sincere had returned home to Atlanta after visiting his mom. He had been happy to see her, but now it was back to the real world. He dreaded the eerie feeling of emptiness that surrounded him as he walked around the house. It was quiet, cold and depressing. Each room he entered held a special memory with Tara, from her infectious laugh to her lingering perfume. His mom was right; everywhere he turned reminded him of her. He made his way into the living room and picked up a photo of them on their wedding day. It was the best day of his life. As the memories came to mind, he wiped away a tear. *Could he really sell the family home? And what about his dad?* He set the photo down of him and Tara and picked up the one of him, his mom and dad smiling for the camera. It was the last time they were all happy together. He still wasn't sure if he was making the right decision, but if he wanted to feel some normalcy again, he knew what had to be done.

Pulling out his laptop, he began to search Realtor-dot-com for the top five realtors in his zip code. He called and talked to the top three and settled on the one he thought was the best fit, Linda Ciardiello from Keller Williams. She was local to the area and available to meet him that afternoon to look over the property. He asked if she'd be able to get rid of the furniture as well. She assured him that wouldn't be a problem because she resold homes all the time. However, it would be his responsibility to take out all the personal items he wanted to keep. Linda had arrived and their meeting went well. Before she left, he had signed the contract.

* * *

Several hours later, Sincere was packing up huge garbage bags, now certain he wanted to give most of Tara's belongings to Goodwill. He took a short break and made him something to eat. Once he was done, he made a brief call to his mom.

"Hi, Ma, I decided to follow your advice. I'm selling the house. Do you want this china cabinet?" he asked. Although, it was bittersweet, she seemed glad to hear he was moving on.

Doreen paused, thinking long and hard about it. Finally, she said, "No, but save the dishes for me. They were passed down to me from your grandma."

"Okay," Sincere agreed. "I'll talk to you later." When they hung up, he started to call Vanessa but changed his mind. He needed to do this alone. He knew Vanessa, and didn't want her to feel guilty or think he felt he was being pressured into making this type of decision. The only problem, they hadn't talked in almost a week. Would she understand why he hadn't called? Or would she assume the relationship was over? He was taking a big risk by not communicating with her.

DOUBTFUL FEELINGS

A few days later, Keith stood at the door of Vanessa's office. Now that a camera was installed, he could envision her standing on the other side deciding on whether or not to open it. Finally, after several long minutes, the door swung open and Vanessa appeared.

Wow this is harder than I thought," he mumbled to himself. She was dressed in a navy-blue blazer with matching slacks, a white silk blouse and three-inch heels. Her natural makeup, fashionable necklace and neatly-styled hair completed the look.

Suddenly, a knot formed in his dry throat. "Hello, Vanessa," he said in a low, casual voice. "I was following up to see how your system was working out. And..." He lowered his head. Her piercing eyes were so intense, it caused him to briefly look away. He forced the words out anyway, "...have you given it some thought, if we could go out?" He inhaled a deep breath as she continued to stare at him.

She blinked out of her trance and said, "Where are my manners?" She stepped to the side to let him enter.

Lisa had taken a personal day to spend time with Antonio. Meanwhile, Vanessa was at the office on her iPad making file folders for her new clients. It had been a rough couple of days because she still hadn't heard from Sincere, and at this point, she didn't know what to think. She knew he was alive from the quick "hey you" text messages, but that was about it.

"Thanks, Keith, for stopping by. The system is working great. No complaints. I have to admit, though, you asking me out the other day caught me by surprise. I'm flattered, but I um..., I'm actually seeing someone." Vanessa bit her bottom lip. Her words didn't sound convincing, even to her.

Keith raised a brow. "Are you just saying that to get rid of me?"

"No, it's complicated..."

"Well you know, if you want to talk about it, I'm a good listener. And it won't cost you much," he added.

For the first time in over a week, Vanessa cracked a smile. "That's very sweet but I'll be alright, it's just that..." She stopped in mid-sentence. She wasn't one to talk openly about her feelings. It felt strange when the roles were reversed.

176

He seemed to know she was contemplating how to answer. "How about we stay right here? On your turf. We can order some lunch and then you can kick me out. This way, I get to see the nice side of you."

Once again Vanessa smiled, agreeing to join him for lunch. They were both familiar with Tsing Tao Chinese Restaurant, a quaint, little place nearby that served quality food. Vanessa ordered the Honey Walnut Shrimp over white rice. Keith had the Sesame Chicken with mixed vegetables delivered by Grubhub.

* * *

"Okay, so now that your stomach is full, tell me why is a pretty woman like you in a complicated relationship?"

She shrugged. "Do you want the short version or the long one?"

"I'll settle for whatever you want to share. Hopefully, by then, it will be time for dinner." He winked at her.

Vanessa laughed. She loved a man with a great sense of humor and who was intelligent. She immediately felt at ease with him as she began to explain her current situation. True to his word, Keith sat quietly and listened.

Finally, he said, "If I'm hearing you correctly, it sounds like you need to cut this guy some slack. I mean, truthfully, it's not always about a woman. Contrary to what society is led to believe, men have feelings too. I know we're taught to be strong. With the weight of the world on our shoulders. We may process things differently. It doesn't necessarily mean we're with another woman. I think this guy just needs a little space and time to figure things out. It wasn't like he was with his wife and things didn't work out. Unfortunately, she died. Then, he met you. You told me you dated him for a while and then you moved. What's up with that? Had it occurred to you that you left him too?

"Listen, I like you, Vanessa, but this whole *what about me?* is played out. Give him a chance. Take it from someone who knows... I've been through a horrendous situation that no one should go through. In order for me to recover from it, it took a long time to heal. Now I'm starting fresh. My mind is clear. I've got everything I need..."

"Not everything." Vanessa gave him a side-eye.

"Well, I'm working on that. But you got issues...so I'll just move on." They both laughed.

"Seriously," Vanessa said. "I would be happy to return the favor if you need someone to talk to."

"Don't try to change the subject. This isn't about me. My point is that depression is real. What may take a guy six months to go through hell and back, it could take the next man over a year. And you being a therapist, if you don't follow your own rules to get better, then it's always going to be there. You have to be able to communicate with each other."

* * *

After talking all day with Keith, night began to fall. Vanessa felt better because she needed to hear this from a man's perspective. She wanted Sincere in her life and knew she had to be patient with him. She believed in her heart that he would come around in due time.

"Thank you, Keith, this was fun. You are something else."

"See, I'm not so bad. Maybe you could introduce me to one of your friends."

Vanessa shook her head. "All the drama you have going on, I don't think so."

"Yeah, you're probably right, I may need to schedule an appointment with you after all."

"That's fine, just know that I charge by the hour," she said, as she walked him to the door.

FALLING FOR YOU

Lisa and Antonio planned their first romantic getaway to Lake Tahoe. It was about a four-hour drive south of Reno, on the border of Nevada and California. Considered one of the most beautiful places in the country with large mountains, crystal clear waters and rustic views. Lisa hadn't been to Lake Tahoe since she was a little girl. Her dad would take her skiing at Heavenly Mountain Ski Resort. She enjoyed riding on the gondola lifts, so she could slide down the slopes in her snow saucer. While her dad would take off on his skis and poles. Her favorite part was meeting him at the bottom. From there they'd go for hot chocolate with marshmallows. Those were the days, she thought back to the sweet memories.

Antonio parked the car at the Marriott's Timber Lodge, which was a beautiful resort in a prime location. It had an array of amenities, lots of activities and was in close proximity to the slopes. After checking in with the front desk staff, they made their way into the spacious one-bedroom villa that had a fireplace, flat screen TV, kitchenette and private bathroom. Once settled, they dropped off their overnight bags and took the complimentary shuttle to the city's district. They booked the Ultimate Adventure Pass: a full day of skiing, indoor rock climbing, hiking tours, eating and shopping. By the time they returned to the room, they were drained.

"This is a nice place," Lisa said. She and Antonio sat by the fire and talked about the day's events. They were snuggled up together on the couch.

"I'm glad you like it." Antonio pulled her closer into his arms. "Can I ask you something?" he asked, breaking into the comfortable silence in the room.

"Anything," she said.

"These past few months have been filled with joy. I love spending time with you, Lisa, so I was wondering," he stroked her hair, "can we make it official? Will you be my girl?" He came right out and asked instead of beating around the bush.

Lisa smiled. "How could I say no to a hot guy like you. Yes, of course, I'll be yours."

That's all he needed to hear. He leaned forward and kissed her. He hadn't felt this happy in a long time. Lisa was a free-spirited person with an extraordinary mind, a beautiful soul that had an unconventional approach towards life. In his heart, he knew she was the *one,* as he continued to stroke her hair, pushing it gently off her forehead. He couldn't have asked for a better girlfriend. They stayed like that, wrapped in each other's arms for at least another hour before heading off to bed.

* * *

The next day, Lisa and Antonio rose early to eat breakfast, check out and then get back on the road. They both agreed it had been a fun-filled weekend. While on the trip, Lisa bought something for Vanessa and wanted to drop it off to her at the office. Upon their arrival, Lisa and Antonio sat talking and kissing in the car for a while.

"Are you sure you don't want me to wait for you?"

"I'll be fine." She steadied her breathing when they pulled apart. "I'm going to see how Vanessa is doing, if she is even here. If not, I'm going to set her gift on her desk and then leave."

"Okay, I had a great time."

"Me too." They kissed one last time before she pulled the door handle and stepped out the car.

* * *

"Hello Lisa," Sarah called out from behind her. Startled by the sound of her voice, Lisa's eyes widened, as she stopped midway inside the door. Antonio had already pulled off, so without hesitation, she quickly pushed the panic button on the silent alarm that alerted the authorities.

"Sarah, what are you doing here?"

"I wanted to see you. You look so beautiful. Is that a new outfit?" Sarah admired her knit sweater dress paired with a black and gold studded leather belt, knee-high boots and cute handbag as she slowly moved toward her.

Stepping back, Lisa's heartbeat began to race, her pulse quickened.

"I miss you, Lisa. Why did you leave me? We worked so well together. But now, I see you with Vanessa, and I don't like it. You know she took you away from me. Is she a better boss than I am? Does she make you work hard? Or stay at work late? *Answer me.*" Sarah raised her voice.

Unable to speak, Lisa's thoughts spun out of control. *Why is she doing this? Is she going to kill me? What should I do?*

Sarah begged and pleaded in a menacing tone. "I want you to come back, that's all. Will you come back? Huh, Lisa?"

Lisa screamed and twisted left when Sarah brandished a knife and lunged at her. Right then, Antonio snuck up from behind Sarah and wrestled the gleaming weapon out of her hand. Thankfully, he'd doubled back when Lisa left something in his car. Driving up, he immediately spotted Lisa in trouble. Sirens were heard approaching in the distance while Antonio pinned her down to the ground until help arrived. Antonio let go of Sarah when the responding officer, who was Officer Williams, quickly jumped out the vehicle and accessed the scene.

"Do you want to press charges?" she asked Lisa, who was visibly shaking.

This time, Lisa didn't hesitate and nodded *yes*. Officer Williams told her she would need to give a written statement down at the station. Sarah was placed under arrest and led away in handcuffs.

* * *

Once the police and bystanders were gone, Antonio and Lisa embraced each other tighter. "Told you to keep me close," he whispered against her ear.

"I'm glad you're here."

"I'm glad it's over, and Sarah won't be following you around anymore." He kissed her face. "Come on, I'll take you to the station." Antonio started walking, but Lisa slowed her pace.

"Antonio?"

"Yes." He stared back at her.

"I love you and was so afraid she would come after you."

He paused for a second, because he already felt the same way about her but had been too afraid to say it first. "I love you, too," he confessed.

Antonio pulled her into his arms and kissed her again. "The sooner we leave, the quicker we can get back, and then you can really show me how much you love me," he joked.

"Whatever," Lisa said, as she rolled her eyes and laughed. They climbed into the car and drove away.

HOME TO STAY

One week later, Vanessa decided to join Lisa, Antonio, Megan and Mike at the Marriott, which was their weekly hangout spot. She still hadn't heard from Sincere, and although everyone was coupled up except her, it felt good to be out.

"Have you seen Sarah?" Megan asked Lisa.

"No, and I hope it stays that way."

Sarah had been charged with aggravated assault. Needless to say, she lost her job and would serve jail time.

"I have enjoyed not having to look over my shoulders every two seconds."

"I know that's right!" Vanessa agreed.

"Look who's talking. You haven't seen Sincere either," Lisa replied.

"Yeah, but at least he's not a stalker," Vanessa defended him.

"You sure about that?"

That voice. Couldn't be. Vanessa quickly turned around in total shock. "Sincere?" she shouted. "Oh my God! What are you doing here?" She jumped up and immediately threw her arms around him and hugged him tight.

"I told you I would be back to see you soon. Surprise!" he said as they all cheered and clapped.

"I can't believe you're here. When did you get here? How long are you staying?"

"Baby, breathe." He kissed her lips. "We have a lot to talk about, but I'm here for as long as you'll have me."

Looking confused by his response, she began to ramble. "But what about Atlanta... your house...your trucking company...?"

Unbeknownst to Vanessa, Sincere had sold his home. He kept his trucking company based in Atlanta and booked a parking rental space to store his truck in San Francisco. He hadn't found a place to live yet, but Antonio offered him short-term housing at the hotel. He didn't want to automatically assume that he would stay with her.

"I'll explain everything to you later," he said, taking a seat next to hers at the table. For now, Sincere was glad that he'd never have to utter the words, *Please Don't Go,* ever again.

Thank you for reading.

The End

"Meet the Author"
Tesa Erven

Tesa Erven rocks the pen when it comes to writing contemporary romance fiction. Bursting onto the publishing scene in 2015, she has already captured a large reading audience with her six-book "The Loose End" series. Tesa's hectic life as a wife and mother of two children, while holding down a full-time job, is the steam that pushes her to create a private world of her own. This realm of unique, real and dramatic love stories is filled with suspense and riddled with plot twists. Escape into the world of this New Jersey romantic that will keep you intrigued and pondering what the next page will bring. You can visit her website at www.tesaerven.com or connect with her on Facebook at

www.facebook.com/authortesaerven